# Landing In A Coffin

## Chad Cartwright

It was a cloudy but rainless day in Laredo, Texas. It was humid but not unbearable. Billy drove his tan Chevy 4x4 truck down the narrow alley behind The Great Wall Chinese restaurant. He was parked only seven blocks away from the Mexican border. His window was rolled down and he was listening to classic rock on The Eagle 106.7 out of San Antonio. The faint smell of polluted Mexican air blowing across the Rio Grande mixing with the overwhelming smell of garbage from the restaurant began to nauseate him. He rolled up his window and turned on the air conditioner. Billy had parked there many times before. In fact, he had been doing this for over a decade now. The Chinese restaurant was a strange place to meet the corrupt police of Laredo who were bringing him another shipment of drugs. He supposed it was as good a cover as any. It was a very unlikely place for a drug deal to go down.

Billy had grown a beard for the first time in his life and it was causing him to itch like crazy. He had a boyish face and was tired of being called "Billy the Kid". He thought the beard might help get rid of the nickname. He looked at his scraggly brown beard in the rearview mirror as he scratched at it.

"I'm going to shave this damn thing off as soon as I get home."

He leaned back and closed his eyes. He thought about how he came to this point in his life.

Billy, Johnathon William Clarke, grew up in South San Antonio. His early life was uneventful. He stayed out of trouble for the most part. He didn't drink. An encounter with a bottle of tequila was his first and last experience with alcohol. The only bad thing he ever did was smoke weed. His best friend, Chris Williams, was a drug dealer in high school. This didn't bother Billy one bit. It meant discounted weed for him.

The summer before their senior year was to start at South San Antonio High School, Chris found out his family was moving to Dallas. His father received a promotion that required him to relocate. Without Chris, there was going to be a void in the high school drug trade. Chris asked Billy if he wanted to take over. Smoking weed was one thing but selling it was another. Billy didn't have much ambition or plans after graduation. His parents wanted him to go to college but he had no interest.

"I ain't the one who can give you the job though. You'll have to interview for it."

"Interview? With who?"

"My supplier. You think these drugs just materialize out of thin air?"

"No. I just never thought about where you got them from. I didn't want to know."

"That's good. In this business, it's better to know as little as possible. So, what do you think? You in?"

Billy paused for a moment.

"Yeah…I'm in."

"Alright. I'll let you know when and where he wants to meet."

"Sounds good."

Chris didn't flash it but Billy knew he made good money dealing drugs. Besides, by dealing it would mean he could get as much weed as he wanted. He told himself he'd do it through his senior year and then stop. His plan was to save as much money as possible to do whatever he wanted once he graduated. He was naïve.

It was just after noon the next day when the phone rang.

"Hello?"

"Billy?"

"Yeah."

"Hey, your parents home?"

"No."

"Alright. We're comin' over."

"OK."

Billy hung up the phone and walked into the kitchen to make a sandwich. Before he could spread mayonnaise on the bread there was a knock at the front door. Billy opened the door and there stood Chris and his future employer. The supplier was a short, stocky Mexican. He wore a wife beater, khakis, and black Converse. His arms and chest were covered in tattoos.

The Mexican walked in without waiting to be invited. Chris followed and shut the door behind him.

"You know who I am?"

"No sir."

"That's the right answer. Anybody asks, you don't know me."

"Yes sir."

"Chris tells me you want to take over for him. Am I right?"

"Yes sir."

"You ever do this kind of work before?"

"No sir."

"You get good grades?"

"Yes sir."

"You drink?"

"No sir."

"Do drugs."

"I smoke weed."

"Ever been arrested?"

"No sir."

"How old are you?"

"Seventeen."

"You think you can handle this?"

"Yes sir."

"We'll see. Who lives here?"

"Just me and my parents."

"They nosey? Get in your business?"

"No sir."

"Good."

"Alright, I'll give you a chance next week. Chris will get you up to speed."

"Thank you."

"Name's Chico. That's all you need to know about me right now. And keep up that 'Yes sir, No sir' shit. I like that."

"Yes sir."

Chico looked at Chris and motioned to the front door with his chin. Chris quickly opened it for him and they stepped outside. Just as Billy was about to close the door, Chico stepped back and placed his left hand against it. The tattoos on his arm stretched as he flexed.

"Remember, I know where you live and I know where your parents live."

He turned and walked away. Billy stared at Chris dumbfounded. Chris just shrugged his shoulders and followed after Chico. Thus began his career.

Billy had come a long way since becoming a pot dealer. He was now a courier. He shuttled drugs from the border to San Antonio for the Mexican mafia. They were known as La Eme, The M. The Mexican mafia had been in existence for over sixty years and to many it was the gang of all gangs.

There was little chance of the police or border patrol catching Billy because the mafia bribed them. He didn't want this job but when "asked" to do it he wasn't about to say no. La Eme doesn't take no for an answer.

As can be imagined, life in the Mexican mafia is very dicey. If the mafia decides you are a threat to the organization you go down for the dirt nap. There is little chance of running for your life or going to the police or feds for protection. Very few of those marked for death are still alive. Those few were in hiding or a maximum security prison. He knew there was no getting out.

Billy opened his eyes. He looked in his rearview mirror and could see the beat up white van backing up to his truck bed. Billy got out and rolled back the cover. Three men, one of them in a police uniform, quickly loaded the tightly packed bundles in the pickup bed and Billy closed the cover. Billy reached in the backseat of his truck and grabbed a black duffel bag. He handed it to the police officer. All this was done in less than a minute without a word being said. The truck and van drove off in opposite directions.

He merged onto I-35 and headed to San Antonio. Billy was waved through the border patrol check station just outside of Laredo. It would take him two and a half hours to get to San Antonio to drop off the drugs. He was driving straight to the Menger Junkyard. This old junkyard is La Eme's central point for drug distribution throughout the United States and even into Canada.

When Billy arrived, he pulled up close to the sheet metal gate. Numerous cameras alerted those inside of his presence. An armed guard pushed the security gate open and Billy drove inside. Half a dozen men appeared and emptied the truck bed. One of the men handed Billy a black duffel bag. It contained one million dollars and a Post-It note was placed on top of the stacks. "Miercoles" was the only word written on it. Today was Sunday so he had a couple days off. He backed out of the junkyard and headed home.

Home was a studio apartment in Southtown, the arts district of San Antonio. Billy had a few friends and a on-again off-again girlfriend in the neighborhood. He claimed to be a trust fund kid and no one questioned it. Billy dabbled in painting and actually sold a few. He was better at it when he wasn't stoned. He didn't drink but he frequented a few bars to socialize. A typical day began with coffee and cereal, a few hits on the bong and a little couch surfing in front of the TV. He wasn't much of a go-getter.

Billy didn't do much during his couple of days off besides shave. He was about to go to bed when his cell phone rang. It was Chris. He was dealing in Dallas and Billy hadn't talked to him in months.

"What's up man?"

"Billy! You alone?"

"Yeah man, what's up?"

"Oh man, I really fucked up! I really fucked up."

"Whoa. Whoa. What are you talking about?"

"I really fucked up. I'm in big trouble man."

"What's going on?"

"I got busted with a lot of coke. The feds offered me a deal and I took it!"

"What?! Are you fucking nuts?! La Eme will kill you!"

"I know! I know! I panicked man.  They said they'd put me away for years, maybe even life."

"You're a dead man.  You're a fucking dead man."

"They want me to wear a wire."

"What?! You get caught with a wire and they will torture you.  You'll pray for death.  Did you give them my name?"

"No way man.  I'd never give you up."

   Billy wasn't so sure.

"Jesus Christ. Damn it Chris!  When La Eme finds out, who do you think is the first person they are going to ask questions?  I'm guilty by association.  Now my life is at risk."

"What do I do?"

"Forget the deal.  Do the time.  You'll be an old man when you get out but at least you'll be alive."

"I'm sorry Billy.  I just panicked.  I don't want to go back to prison."

   There was a moment of silence then Billy sighed.

"Good luck Chris."

"Take care Billy."

   As Chris hung up the recorder stopped.  Chris had already flipped and the DEA was listening.  Billy was right to be suspicious.

   He wondered if La Eme would believe he wasn't involved even if they gave him a chance to plead his case.

   Billy didn't get much sleep that night. He woke up about 3:00 am Wednesday morning and couldn't go back to sleep.  Billy made some coffee and then drove to Nuevo Laredo.  There was a panaderia just around the corner from The Great Wall that made his favorite mango empanadas.  Billy stopped there to get a couple of the delicious Mexican pastries just as they were coming out of the oven.  He also bought a fresh cup of coffee before parking in the alley.  After savoring the flavor of the empanadas, Billy blew on the scalding hot coffee to get a sip.  He leaned back and closed his eyes.  Fatigue was setting in.  Billy dozed off just long enough for his grip to loosen on the cup of coffee.  But when the hot coffee spilled on his crotch he was wide awake.

"Son of a bitch!"

   He pulled some napkins out of his center console and tried to pat himself dry.

"Shit."

Billy glanced up and saw a white Ford Bronco like the one OJ made his slow speed getaway in. It was parked perpendicular to the alley, blocking his exit. He recognized the man in the passenger seat. It was one of the many corrupt policemen of Laredo but he was not in uniform.

He glanced in his rearview mirror. The delivery van was backing up to his truck bed. The red brake lights flashed as the van jerked to a stop. The rear doors swung open and three men armed with machine guns jumped out.

The gunmen opened fire as Billy ducked for cover, put his truck in reverse and floored it. Bullets ripped through the tailgate and the truck windows shattered. He ran over one gunman and pinned the other two against the back of the van. The corrupt policeman in the Bronco was spraying the front of Billy's truck with bullets. Billy grabbed the bag, opened his door and made a mad dash down the alley past the van. The whiplashed driver of the van saw Billy run by. The driver quickly shifted the van into drive and hit the gas. As Billy reached the end of the alley, he ran to the right. The van just missed him and t-boned a mechanic driving his prized black El Camino.

The Bronco made a quick U-turn and then a left turn. It fishtailed and hit a rusted red Chevy Nova parked on the street. Billy continued running and when he got to the intersection he could see the Bronco peeling out. It was headed straight for him.

He kept running and could hear the screech of tires as the Bronco turned the corner following him. There were cars up ahead stopped at a red light. Without even looking, Billy dashed into the street and across the intersection narrowly being missed by the honking traffic.

The driver of the Bronco honked incessantly for the other cars to get out of his way when the light turned green. It was too late. Billy got away.

He worked his way through side streets and alleys. Billy saw a used car dealership and hurried inside. It was just past 9:00 am and Martinez Motors had just opened for business.

He was sweaty and disheveled. He tried to catch his breath as he stared outside.

"Can I help you, senor?"

Billy almost jumped out of his skin. He dropped the bag put his hand over his heart as he turned to see a short fat Mexican with a very thin comb over of jet black hair and a pencil thin mustache. He wore a long sleeve white shirt and a black tie. Black suspenders held up his shiny silver pants that loomed over his black patent leather shoes.

"Shit, you scared me."

He exhaled.

"Yes, sir. I need a vehicle."

"Si. What kind of vehicle, senor?"

"One that can't be traced…Understand?"

"Si. But that costs more money and is hard to come by."

"Si. Do you have anything?"

"Follow me."

Senor Martinez seemed to have some experience with this sort of thing. Billy picked up the bag and followed him out the back door, through a garage and into an open lot fenced with razor wire. There were all sorts of old cars.

"Do any of these actually run?"

"Some do. Ah, here's a good one."

"Which one?"

"Este. El coche anaranjado."

"The orange car? You can't be serious. I'll stick out like a sore thumb."

"It's very reliable. Air cooled engine. Plus convertible."

"No. I want something else."

"This is all I have for you, senor. It runs well and has no VIN number. Take it or leave it."

"Shit. What kind of car is this? It's tiny."

"It's a Volkswagen Karmann Ghia."

"Carmengia?"

"Si. Karmann Ghia."

"What size engine does it have?"

"Mil Seiscientos."

"1600?...ccs?

"Si."

"Can she even go 55 miles an hour?"

"Oh yes."

"Oh yes, with a tailwind going downhill!"

Billy was dejected and desperate. He didn't have time to car shop.

"How much?"

"Cincuenta mil."

"Fifty thousand dollars!? Are you kidding me? No way. I'll pay twenty five."

"Cuarenta."

"Treinta."

"Treinta y cinco."

"Deal. But it's highway robbery. If I can get her to 55 she'll probably rattle apart. One more thing. You never saw me. Understand?"

"Si, senor."

Billy pulled out of the back lot in his orange getaway car. He headed north on Highway 83 to Uvalde. She made it to 55 without falling apart.

The countryside was littered with oil derricks and pump jacks. The oil boom was back on. When he reached Uvalde, he took Highway 55 to Sonora. He stopped there to get gas. There was a problem though.

"How the hell do you fill this thing with gas?"

There was no place for a gas cap. Billy looked in the glove box for an owner's manual but it had been missing for years.

"Where is it?"

Billy thought for a moment.

"Maybe it's on the engine. After all, it's basically a lawnmower."

He opened the engine lid and peered inside. No gas cap. He slammed the lid shut.

"Damn it!"

"Well, if the engine is in the back maybe the gas is in the front."

Billy reached under the dash and pulled the latch release. He walked to the front of the car and opened the bonnet. There it was.

"Finally!"

Billy unscrewed the large gas cap with "VW" embossed across it. When he finished filling it up, he had only added 12 gallons.

"I'm not going to make it anywhere fast on 12 gallons at a time."

Billy had to move fast. He had to get as far away as possible. He took a deep breath and tried to calm himself. Billy began to think over his situation and how he could improve it. Did La Eme think he still posed enough of a threat to hunt him down? If so, they would send Tortuga after him. The thought sent a shiver down his spine.

Tortuga is Spanish for tortoise. It is the nickname of Juan Pedro Jimenez. It's hard to say whether the nickname or simply the name Juan Pedro instills more fear in his prey.

Juan Pedro grew up in the poorest part of Monterrey, Nuevo Leon, Mexico. Monterrey is a city of approximately one million people. It is the last major city before the Texas border. At the border, the city of Nuevo Laredo stares across the Rio Grande at her sister city, Laredo. From Laredo, it's a straight shot to San Antonio. Monterrey is the staging point for drug transportation into the United States.

La Eme recruits many inhabitants of Monterrey into their organization. Juan Pedro was one of those many. Growing up in the housing projects of Monterrey was no fairy tale and Juan Pedro was at the bottom of the pecking order. He had a different nickname as a child. He was known as "Juan Pequeno" and was constantly abused by the larger and stronger street kids. It is hard to believe that someone who instills such fear into friends and foes alike was once a victim himself.

One of the pastimes for the down and out children of Monterrey was sneaking into movie theatres. With no money, sneaking in was the only way they were able to see movies. Sneaking in to see Bruce Lee's "Enter the Dragon" changed his life. He saw how Lee was able to use his skills and techniques to take on and defeat a stronger opponents.

Juan Pedro continued to sneak into theatres to see martial arts movies. Bruce Lee's were his favorite but he watched them all. He wanted to learn as much as he could from anyone who had skills. He also read martial arts books from the local biblioteca to further educate himself.

Every day he practiced the punches, kicks and blocks he saw in the movies. All of his practice began to pay off. Each time he found himself in a fight, he got better. His fights began to end in draws when he was at least able to wear his opponents down. Eventually, he began to win and ultimately he became unbeatable.

His prowess did not go unnoticed by La Eme. He was recruited as an enforcer. For the first time in his life, Juan Pedro had money and a clean place to live. He also had access to a gym and weapons. He learned how to use knives and guns as well as he could use his fists. He was a lethal weapon.

It was as if he could see his opponent's next move and was able to strike first. No one was strong enough or fast enough to beat him. He worked out daily, ate healthy and never drank. His endurance was incredible. He soon became the most feared man in La Eme.

On Saturday nights, cock fights and boxing matches provide entertainment in Monterrey. Sometimes, they are at the same venue. One Saturday, Juan Pedro wash challenged to fight three boxing matches in a row against three different boxers. He accepted without hesitation.

Boxing is considered a major sport in Mexico. It has produced more champions than any other country. Juan Pedro knew he would be fighting worthy opponents.

The first opponent didn't make it through the second round. The second opponent didn't make it through the first. The third boxer was a surprise to Juan Pedro and the growing crowd on hand. The crowd erupted when the last opponent entered the ring. It was Rodolfo Cesar Zarate, the former Mexican Heavyweight Champion.

It was a set up. La Eme "requested" Zarate come to Monterrey to fight Juan Pedro. They knew how tough and capable Juan Pedro was and weren't afraid to pit him against the best. Even if Zarate won, it would show Juan Pedro was able to fight one of the best boxers in all of Mexico. Besides, everyone knew who would win if Zarate and Juan Pedro were to meet in a dark alley.

La Eme told Zarate not to take it easy on Juan Pedro and he didn't. The bell rang and Zarate went to work on Juan Pedro. The crowd was shocked to see Zarate land punch after punch as Juan Pedro struggled to keep pace. Juan Pedro had not been hit so many times and so hard since he was known as Juan Pequeno. The first round ended with Juan Pedro slowly walking back to his corner with a bloody nose and swelling around his left eye. He dropped onto the stool and grabbed a water bottle. He stared across the ring at Zarate while flooding his mouth with water. The bell rang and the second round started. Juan Pedro stood up and squint his eyes at Zarate. He had a plan.

Round after round he followed his plan. He would deliver a flurry of punches to start a round and then put his back against the ropes. Protecting himself with his gloves and moving side to side and back and forth, he made it to the end of each round. Word of the fight got around town and the crowd soon swelled beyond capacity.

Towards the end of the eleventh round, Juan Pedro threw a couple of low punches which infuriated the already frustrated Zarate. Zarate let loose on Juan Pedro and caught him with an uppercut knocking Juan Pedro to the canvas. The bell rang as he landed. Shaking out the cobwebs, Juan Pedro stumbled back to his corner. Zarate dropped onto his stool breathing heavily. His head was cocked to his right side and his mouth was wide open trying to suck in as much air as possible. His arms hung by his side. His opponent across the ring was sitting up straight with controlled breathing and arms resting on his legs. The bell rang and the twelfth round started as the others had. Juan Pedro delivered a flurry of punches but this time he did not stop. Now Zarate was against the ropes and after a few more punches he lay unconscious. The crowd went wild. They jumped into the ring and hoist Juan Pedro on their shoulders.

Juan Pedro watched Muhammad Ali beat George Foreman with the rope-a-dope and he used it to beat Zarate. The tortoise had beaten the hare. La Eme was very pleased. The legend of Tortuga was born.

Now, Billy was the hare.

Billy merged onto Interstate 10 and headed west. He took the next exit at Ozona and headed north along Highway 137. When he reached Lamesa, he took Highway 87 to Lubbock. He pulled into the first gas station. This time he knew where the gas cap was.

There is no air conditioner in a Karmann Ghia. Billy didn't want to drop the top but going 55 with two windows down was not working. He unlatched the top, folded it back and snapped the boot over it. He cleaned the windshield and headed into town.

Billy merged onto I-27 headed for Amarillo as smoke began pouring out the back of the Ghia. The engine began to sputter and he was losing speed.

"No, No, No."

He took the exit onto 50ᵗʰ Street and turned left on the overpass. He continued down 50ᵗʰ Street scanning the neighborhood for a place to get the Ghia off the street. As he reached Avenue Q, he saw the Koko Inn Motel and pulled into the parking lot. He drove around the motel and parked in the back. The Ghia died as he pulled into a parking spot.

"Shit. Well, this is great."

He got out of the car and put the top up. He rolled up the windows, grabbed the bag and locked the doors. Billy surveyed his surroundings. The parking lot was more than half empty. Older model cars and trucks that had seen better days filled random parking spots. Billy made his way to the front desk.

A morbidly obese woman with a lazy eye and a jack o' lantern smile was sitting there.

"Hello, ma'am."

"Well, howdy stranger. How are you?"

"Fine and yourself."

"Just livin' the dream. What can I do for ya'?"

"I need a room for the night, maybe two."

"That ain't gonna be a problem, honey. We got plenty of rooms. We even got some of them beds with magic fingers. You want a room with one of them beds?"

"Thank you ma'am, but that won't be necessary."

"I'll give you a room on the second floor. It'll be quieter."

"Thank you."

Billy paid, went outside and climbed the stairs to his room. He stood in front of the door and put the key in the door knob. Billy looked to see if anyone was watching him before he turned the key and stepped in quickly. He closed the door, locked the door knob and the chain door lock in less than a second. He rest his forehead against the door and exhaled.

Billy turned around to survey his penthouse suite. It was a musty room and smelt of cigarettes. The queen size bed had a cheap green and yellow comforter on it. There was a nightstand with an ashtray, a lamp and a coin acceptor with the words "Magic Fingers" written on it. Next to the door was a dresser that didn't match the nightstand. On top of the dresser sat a black and white TV.

Billy didn't care. He fell on the bed clutching his bag of drug money and fell asleep.

It was dark outside when Billy woke up in a panic. He was sweating. The room was dark. A faint light shone through the thin curtains.

He lay his head down on the cheap comforter covering the bed, rolled on his back, took a deep breath and slowly exhaled.

"If only it was a nightmare…"

He sighed and sat up.

"Well? What now, Billy the Kid?"

Billy strolled over to the window and looked through the curtains. There was no one there. He closed them tight and walked over to the side of the bed. Billy bent over to turn the lamp on and sat down. He reached in his pocket and pulled out his dugout.

He packed the end of the faux cigarette tight with his high potency weed. After a few hits he began to feel better. He knew paranoia might creep up on him, especially given the circumstances, but he was willing to take the risk. Billy needed to calm his nerves and not care for a little while.

Billy lay down and closed his eyes. He felt the room spinning. His skin tingled and he pictured himself at home painting. A strange shadow appeared on the curtains. It looked like a pterodactyl. He stood up and walked to the window. The pterodactyl flapped his wings and shook his head. Billy slowly opened the curtains and looked out the window. There sat a Blue Jay. He chirped at Billy and flew away. Billy chuckled. It was drug-induced but at least it was a laugh. Billy needed it.

He crawled under the bed with the duffel bag and ripped open the fabric covering the underside of the box spring mattress. Billy stuffed the bag inside the frame and tucked in the torn fabric. He crawled out from under the bed and stood up. Then he knelt down to look under the bed making sure there was no fabric hanging down in case anyone was to look there.

Billy walked to the bathroom and laughed at his reflection. His eyes were already bloodshot. He turned on the cold water in the sink and splashed his face with it. The towel he used to dry his face was questionably clean. Billy stumbled to the door and unlocked the chain and knob. He put his hand on the door knob, took a deep breath, slowly exhaled and opened the door.

Billy saw a McDonald's on the way to his five-star hotel in his classic car. He walked to the end of the block and got a Big Mac, large fries, and a large Coke to go. He stopped at a 7-Eleven and got a chocolate bar before returning to his room. Billy checked to see if the money was still in the box spring then he scarfed down his food. A couple of empanadas were not enough food to get him through the day.

He grabbed his dugout and took a few more hits before turning on the TV. The nightly news was just starting.

"Good evening and thank you for joining us. We have breaking news out of San Antonio today. The DEA has raided a junkyard in south San Antonio and made numerous arrests. Sources tell us that the Menger Junkyard in San Antonio was being used to traffic drugs by the Mexican mafia known as 'La Eme'. This is the largest drug bust in Texas history."

"Oh, shit."

There was video footage of gang members being arrested. Billy knew some of them. There were also clips of surveillance videos. Billy was in one of them. Thankfully, he was wearing a baseball hat and had his scraggly beard.

The DEA knew who he was but thought he was most likely dead. Tortuga knew he wasn't dead though.

Juan Pedro had paid a visit to Martinez Motors. He didn't believe Senor Martinez when he denied selling a car to a nervous gringo. Once Senor Martinez' head was in a vice and his right eye popped out of it's socket, he remembered. Juan Pedro thanked him for the information, pulled out his knife and slit Senor Martinez' throat. He calmly walked out of the garage. Juan Pedro didn't think it would be too hard to find an orange Karmann Ghia and he knew going north was the only way Billy could escape.

Billy turned the TV off, grabbed his dugout and took a long hit. He turned off the lamp and lay down. The DEA knew his name, Juan Pedro was after him and he was on foot. He didn't get much sleep that night.

He got up in the morning and booked another room for the night. His next stop was at 7-Eleven. Billy bought a large coffee, a newspaper and a trucker hat.

When he got back to his room, he flipped open the paper. La Eme was front page news. Billy read the article.

"Confidential informant, huh? Wonder who that could be?"

Billy closed the paper and set it on the bed next to him. He grabbed his dugout and took another hit. He glanced at the name of the newspaper.

"Lubbock Avalanche-Journal ? Avalanche? Are you kidding me? What a dumbass name for a newspaper in Lubbock, Texas. This is the flattest place on earth. Where the hell is an avalanche going to come from?"

Billy pushed the paper on the floor. He let out a big sigh and pressed his palms against his forehead and closed his eyes. When he opened his eyes, he noticed the paper was open to the classifieds. He picked it up and glanced at the ads. He thought for a moment. Maybe laying low here for a while wouldn't be such a bad idea. No one would expect him to stay here. Let the heat die down and then make his escape.

Staying in a motel room was too dangerous. He needed an apartment or a rent house but they would require rental history, references and identification.

"That won't work. Hhm, I'll have to think about that."

He needed to find a car but that could wait if he was able to hide out for a while. Billy picked up the paper and browsed through the ads. One caught his attention.

…"Help wanted. Need caretaker for elderly gentleman. Room and board provided. Please call 806-555-5309."…

Room and board provided.  Those words caught his attention.

"Perfect."

Billy ripped out the ad and rushed to the pay phone at the 7-Eleven.  He dialed the number and cleared his throat as he anxiously waited for someone to answer.

"Nixon residence."

It was a pleasant elderly woman's voice.

"Yes ma'am.  I was calling about the help-wanted ad in the paper."

"Oh, good.  Do you have experience?

"Oh, yes ma'am.  In fact, I took care of my grandfather when he was dying of cancer."

"Oh, dear.  I am so sorry for your loss."

"It's alright.  He's with the Lord now."

"Well, this might be a perfect fit for you.  You see, it's my older brother who needs help.  He can't get around very well anymore.  Now, I warn you, he is not the easiest man to get along with.  He's gone through a number of caretakers."

"Well, I get along with almost everyone so that shouldn't be a problem."

"What is your name young man?"

"It's John…"

He couldn't give his real name and he hadn't thought of an alias to use.

"John?"

"Yes, John.  Uh, John Smith."

"Alright, Mr. Smith.  Can you meet me at his house this afternoon, say about 2:30?"

"Yes ma'am.  I sure can."

Billy got the address from Ms. Nixon.  Before leaving 7-Eleven, he got a burrito, a large Coke and a chocolate bar.  He went back to his room, ate and took a few hits before taking a shower.

He smelt better and felt better afterwards but needed some clean clothes.  Ms. Nixon's brother didn't live far.  He lived on 37th Street so at least Billy knew which direction to head and didn't have to ask anyone for directions.  Maybe he could find a clothing store along the way.  Billy took a thin stack of $100 dollar bills out of the duffel bag and stuffed them deep into his front pocket.  He hid the bag and set off for his job interview, the second of his life.

Luckily for Billy, there was a Target along the way.  Billy got some nice clothes, dress shoes, a belt and toiletries.  He paid for everything, went into the restroom, cleaned himself up and changed into his new duds.  He continued his walk and arrived at his destination five minutes early.

It was a modest red brick home in a decent neighborhood.  A white Cadillac Eldorado was parked in the single car driveway.  Billy walked up the front door and rang the doorbell.  The screen door had a large "N" in the middle of it.

Ms. Nixon answered the door.  She was a frail elderly woman with a head of white back combed hair.

"Mr. Smith!  So nice to meet you.  Please, come in."

The house smelled of old people.

"Please, call me John."

"Alright John, I am Margaret Nixon.  Please follow me and I'll introduce you to my brother.  Now remember, he's a grumpy old man so you have to be patient with him."

"No problem."

Billy followed Ms. Nixon through the living room.  There wasn't much to see.  There was a very large and very old television sitting on thick brown carpet.  It faced an oval wooden coffee table and a well-worn olive drab couch.  There were random pictures hanging on the faux-wood panel walls.  Some were black and white and some were color.

They entered the kitchen.  The kitchen had a lovely white, yellow and green color scheme.  Ms. Nixon's brother sat hunched over in his wheelchair at a dilapidated card table.  There was a bottle of Black Velvet whiskey and a small glass in front of him.  He was a very frail looking old man.  He wore a flannel shirt, a pair of brown pants, white socks and black orthopedic Velcro shoes.  His gray hair was thin and long.  He would have looked better with his hair cut short or even shaved.  The most notable things were his glasses.  They were large black rimmed glasses with thick square lenses that magnified the size of his brown eyes.  Billy could only think of Harry Caray when he looked at him.  He tried not to laugh.

"Who the hell is this?"

"Carwood!  Be polite.  This is Mr. John Smith."

"John Smith?  That's a very generic name, Mr. John Smith."

"Yes sir.  It is."

Billy extended his hand and Carwood shook it.

"Well, have a seat."

Ms. Nixon sat to the right of Carwood and Billy to his left.

"It's nice to meet you Mr. Nixon."

"Uh, huh."

"Mr. Smith…"

"Please, Ms. Nixon, call me John."

"Alright, John has personal experience as a caretaker. He helped take care of his grandfather who had cancer."

"Well, I don't have cancer."

"Mr. Smith, I mean John, is a nice young man and I think you should give him a chance."

"You do, huh? Well, John, how long did your grandfather live while in your care?"

"About a year."

"If you can keep me comfortable for a year without being too much of a nuisance, you've got yourself a deal."

Carwood extended his hand and Billy shook it.

"Deal."

Ms. Nixon quietly clapped her hands and asked when Billy could start.

"Tomorrow."

"Excellent. Tomorrow it is."

"Yeah…excellent."

"Well, I'll see you tomorrow, Mr. Nixon."

Carwood just sighed.

Billy and Ms. Nixon walked to the front door.

"I'll bring some groceries over once a week and give you some time to get out of the house. Oh! We completely forgot to discuss your salary. It's free room and board and a hundred dollars a week. Is that satisfactory?"

"Yes ma'am."

"Well, as you can tell, you're going to earn every penny. See you tomorrow. Is eight o'clock alright?"

"Yes ma'am. See you then."

Billy walked out the front door and breathed a sigh of relief. He walked a block away, pulled out his dugout and took a big hit. He went back to Target and bought a suitcase, new wardrobe and more toiletries. This would be his last night at the Koko Inn.

Billy arrived at 8:00am the next morning. Margaret Nixon was already there. She was unloading groceries from the trunk of her Eldorado. Billy put down his suitcase but kept the duffel bag strapped across his torso and helped her.

"Good morning John. How are you?"

"Fine, thank you. And yourself?"

"Fine, thank you. Carwood is in the living room watching TV."

"One of my favorite pastimes."

Once the groceries were put away, Ms. Nixon showed Billy to his room. It was a small plain room with a queen size bed and a dresser. Billy shoved his duffel bag on the top shelf of the closet. He received his final instructions from Ms. Nixon and she left for the week.

Carwood sat in his wheelchair in front of the TV watching the morning news. Billy sat down on the couch.

"How are you today, Mr. Nixon."

"I'm dyin'."

"Is there anything I can do for you?"

"Yeah, yard work."

"Yard work?"

"Yeah, go mow the yard. Lawnmower is in the shed."

"OK."

Mowing the lawn was better than awkwardly sitting next to the old man. There wasn't much to mow. The yard was mostly dead and the tallest thing in it was weeds.

Lunch consisted of bologna sandwiches and original Dr Pepper in small glass bottles. There was no conversation and Carwood went to his room and took a nap afterwards. Billy grabbed his dugout and went to the backyard. This was the last of his weed. He smoked and wondered where he could get some more. It was too risky to buy some off a hoodlum on a street corner. If he got arrested the DEA would find him. He'd just have to do without.

"This sucks. No more weed and I'm under house arrest with Mr. Grumpy Butt."

The next few days were pretty much the same. Carwood had Billy doing chores while he watched TV and napped. Ms. Nixon came to the house at the end of the week and Billy couldn't leave fast enough.

He walked over to Target and bought some books, magazines, a cd player and cds to keep himself entertained while being under house arrest. He didn't know how long he could keep up the charade. Billy was stir-crazy but he knew it was better than being dead or in prison.

When Billy returned, Ms. Nixon cornered him and asked how things were going.

"Fine, Ms. Nixon. Just fine."

"Oh, good! That makes me feel so good to hear that. Carwood can be so difficult sometimes. I was worried about you two."

"Nothing to worry about Ms. Nixon. How was your week?"

"Oh, busy, busy. Well, if you ever need anything, you've got my number. Please don't hesitate to call me."

"Thank you Ms. Nixon."

"I almost forgot. Here's you first week's pay."

She handed him a check.

"Would it be alright to get paid in cash? I don't have a checking account."

"Certainly. I'm afraid I don't have any cash on me. Would it be alright to pay you next week?"

"Certainly."

"John, I am so glad I found you. You are such a pleasant young man. I hope some of you rubs off on Carwood. "

She headed for the front door.

"See you next week."

"Bye."

Billy turned around and went into the living room. Carwood was asleep in his wheelchair and The Price is Right was on TV. The couch creaked as Billy sat down. The sound startled Carwood.

"Jesus Christ boy! Don't sneak up on me."

"Sorry Mr. Nixon. How are you feeling today."

"A little jumpy."

Billy turned to look at the random pictures that were on the living room wall. There were black and white pictures of men in uniform. Some of the pictures were of men parachuting and there were strange looking gliders being pulled by large planes.

"We're you in the military Mr. Nixon?"

"Nope. I stole all those pictures and hung 'em on my wall. Yes, I was in the military."

Billy shrugged off Carwood's attitude.

"Did you fight in a war?"

"Yep. World War Two."

"Wow. Where did you fight?"

"Europe."

"What was it like?"

"Bad. Very bad."

Billy left it at that. They finished watching The Price is Right without any further conversation. As the show ended, Billy stood up.

"Well, I saw some weeds in the alley so I'm going to get to work."

Carwood didn't say anything.

Billy finished pulling the weeds and came inside the house to make lunch for himself and Carwood. Carwood had already eaten and gone to his room for a nap.

"Lunch and a siesta sounds like a good idea."

He ate lunch and headed to his room for a nap.

Carwood rolled into the kitchen late that afternoon. Billy was making dinner.

"Don't take too long with that dinner. Tonight is the first night of Monday Night Football."

"It's spaghetti, so it won't take long."

"Alright, then."

After washing the dishes, Billy joined Carwood in the living room to watch the game.

"Who's playing?"

"The Broncos and the Giants."

"Should be a good game."

"Well, I wish the Cowboys were playin'."

Carwood fell asleep before halftime. Billy started to help him to his room but Carwood was having none of it.

"I can get myself to bed!"

The next morning Billy made bacon and eggs for breakfast.

"Who won the game last night?"

"Denver, 31 to 20."

"Hhm."

As Billy was washing the dishes, he heard the TV volume getting louder and louder. He left the dirty dishes in the sink and walked into the living room. On the screen was the World Trade Center with smoke billowing out one of the towers. The newscasters were speculating on what happened. There were numerous reports that a plane flew into the side of the building.

Billy stood motionless with his mouth agape. He, as anyone else in front of a TV at that moment, will never forget the horrific sight of smoke billowing out of the first tower as a plane came into view from the side of the television screen. He couldn't, no one could believe it. There wasn't time to process what was about to happen. How could such a thing happen? But it did. The plane flew directly into the second tower.

A massive jet-fueled fireball exploded out of the other side of the second tower. The plane was no more. Now both towers were ablaze.

"A second plane has just hit the other tower. I can't believe it. A second plane has just crashed into the other tower. Right before our eyes. Ladies and gentlemen, this is no accident."

Why is it we remember where we were and what we were doing at such moments?

Billy's parents remember exactly where they were when Oswald assassinated Kennedy and when Armstrong took one small step for man and one giant leap for mankind. He was a smart-ass kid in elementary school when the principal announced over the school intercom that Reagan had been shot. In junior high, he was in the cafeteria line waiting for a slice of pizza when his science teacher told him the Space Shuttle exploded.

Now, he will never forget standing in front of a very old television set in the home of a dying World War II veteran expecting to see the morning news or a game show but instead seeing the largest attack ever on mainland America.

"Damn!...It's just like Pearl."

He turned to see Carwood focused on the television screen.

"Just like Pearl Harbor."

He shook his head back and forth.

"I can't believe it. I never thought it could happen again."

Carwood lowered his head. He had seen enough. He backed his wheel chair into the kitchen and went straight for the Black Velvet.

Billy followed him into the kitchen as Carwood pulled the bottle out of the bottom cabinet and grabbed two glasses. He poured himself and Billy a glass.

"I don't drink."

"You will damn well have a drink with me today!"

Billy motioned to the TV.

"Don't you want to watch this? What if something else happens?"

"No! I don't!"

Billy sat at the table. Carwood raised his elbow high and his fingers brushed the table as he pushed the glass to Billy with the back of his fingers. It looked more like an ape motion that a human one.

"I've seen enough."

Carwood raised his glass with his right hand. He grimaced as the pain from his long ago fractured collar bone reminded him he should have used his left hand.

"A toast."

"To what?"

"To those who died today."

Billy raised his glass with his right hand and tapped his glass against the glass of the dying old man who sat across from him. He took a sip and winced as it burned his throat. He unsuccessfully tried to not cough. Carwood took a large gulp and poured himself another drink.

"I suppose wars will never end. The best men are the ones who get killed. It's a shame…a damn shame. Another toast."

Billy raised his glass.

"To?"

"To…the next pointless war, I suppose."

They each took a drink. Billy was able to keep from coughing this time. Carwood became silent and lowered his head. Billy went back into the living room to watch the coverage. He learned about the hijacked planes, the crash in Pennsylvania and the attack on the Pentagon. Carwood stayed in the kitchen and drank.

The coffee was ready and Billy was making an omelette when Carwood rolled into the kitchen the next morning. Yesterday, Billy had to help Carwood to bed after finding him passed out drunk on the kitchen table. He seemed no worse for wear which surprised Billy.

"Could use some coffee if you don't mind."

"Yes sir."

Billy promptly filled a coffee cup and sat it down in front of him.

"Thank you."

"You're welcome. Omelette sound good, Mr. Nixon?"

"Yes. Thank you."

"I'll make some toast as well."

That was the last of the conversation until Carwood finished his breakfast. Billy started to stand up and clear the table.

"Tell me about yourself, John."

Billy sat back with a puzzled look on his face. That was the first time he referred to Billy by name.

"Well, there's not much to tell Mr. Nixon."

"Call me Carwood, please."

"Alright."

"Where are you from?"

"I grew up in the…uh…Dallas…area."

"You must be a Cowboys fan as well."

"Yes Sir!"

"What is your last name, John…?

"Smith."

"John Smith. Oh, yes. Generic sounding name. John Smith from the Dallas area. What area, John?"

"Arlington, near Six Flags."

"I see."

"What do your parents do?"

"Well, my mother stayed at home and my father was a salesman."

"Salesman? What kind of salesman? Encyclopedias? Vaccums?

"No. He was a drug rep, a pharmaceutical rep. He visited doctor's offices and such."

"And such. Did you go to college?"

"No sir."

"How did you get to be a caretaker?"

"I took care of my grandfather when he had cancer."

"Yes, I remember you saying that. What kind of cancer?"

"Lung cancer."

"Was he a smoker?"

"Yes sir."

"Do you smoke?"

"No sir."

"Are you sure?"

"Yes, I'm sure."

"I haven't smelled it lately but I have smelled smoke on you before. "

Carwood leaned forward and squinted at him through his Harry Cary glasses.

"Most of my body may be failing me but I still have a keen sense of smell. It doesn't smell like cigarettes either."

Billy didn't reply. There was a long awkward moment of silence.

"I know you're no caretaker either. I've run enough of em' off to know what they're like. You have no medical training and don't even know how to wipe your own ass. So, who are you?"

"I'm no one. No one important. No one dangerous."

"Is John Smith your real name?"

"No sir."

"Why didn't you use your real name?"

"I'm on the run."

"From who?

"The Mexican mafia and the DEA."

Carwood laughed.

"Sounds like you are in a heap of trouble."

"Yes sir. I am."

"Well, maybe we can help each other out."

"How so?"

"I'm dying and I don't want to sit in this house and rot. I'm ready to see the world again, one last time."

"What do you mean?"

"I mean I want to get the hell out of here and I can't do it by myself."

"What's in it for me?"

"You need to get away from here, don't you? Probably out of the country?"

"Yes sir."

"Ever been to Europe?"

"No sir."

"Well, that's where I want to go and I'll help you get there if you help me."

"How?"

"You're about the same age my grandson would be and could pass for him if you wore glasses or grew a beard or put on a wig or something. I still have his passport. We could pose as grandfather and grandson. It could work."

"Well…yesterday, while you were trying to get to the bottom of that bottle of Black Velvet, I was watching the news all day. Every plane in America was grounded. They're going to be very careful about who they let on a plane anymore. I can't fly out of the country and I can't go to Mexico. Canada is my only option."

"Canada, eh? Mighty cold in Canada. You ever been there?"

"No."

"Tell you what. I'll get you farther away than Canada. You get me where I want to go and I'll get you a new identity. I'll pay you too. Many Europeans speak English. You could start a new life there."

"What about your sister? She's going to be a little worried when she finds her brother and his caretaker have vanished."

"Well, that's a chance we'll have to take. If we left after she dropped off the weekly groceries, we'd at least have a seven day head start."

"And if I say no?"

"I can make a phone call and turn you in but that's not what I want to do. I'm the best chance you've got."

"Sounds like I don't have much of a choice."

"No. You don't."

"Can I see the passport?"

Carwood spun around and sped off to his room. Billy could hear drawers being opened and rummaged through. He leaned forward putting his elbows on the table and resting his chin in his palms and his fingers on his temples. Staring at his dirty plate, he couldn't believe what the old man wanted him to do

"Aha! Got it!"

Carwood wheeled back into the kitchen. He was out of breath.

"Here…found it."

Billy opened the passport and turned it sideways. He did not resemble the old man's grandson.

"Are you kidding me? We don't look alike."

"Grow a beard, put on some glasses, wear a wig, whatever."

"This thing expires in less than a month!"

"We need to leave as soon as possible then."

"Shit."

"And you're right. It's too dangerous to fly out of the US. Canada's too far away and they'll tighten security there as well. We'll have to fly out of Mexico."

"Mexico?! Are you nuts? I can't go to Mexico! Did you not just hear me? I'm wanted by the Mexican mafia!"

"They won't expect you to go to Mexico. It's our best chance of getting on a plane. And I'm not interested in going on a cruise with you. I had to cross the Atlantic twice on a boat already and I'm not doing it again!"

" And how are we supposed to get to Mexico?"

"Drive."

"Drive what?"

"My grandson's car."

"Where is it?"

"In the garage. Come on, I'll show you."

Carwood pushed his wheelchair into the laundry room, leaned forward and pushed open the door to the garage. He looked back at Billy and smiled.

"There she is."

Billy peered into the garage as he drug his hand along the inside of the door frame feeling for a light switch. He turned on the light. Everything in the garage was covered in dust. The garage walls were lined with shelves. The shelves were overflowing with paint cans, boxes of nails and screws, tools and a lot of junk. In the middle of the garage, a car was covered with a large paint tarp. Billy grabbed the corner of the tarp and pulled it back. Billy stared at the car.

"No. No way."

"What?"

"I'm not driving that car."

"Why not?"

"Because that's what got me stuck here in the first place!"

"Well, if it makes you feel any better, I don't like it either but this isn't the time for car shopping."

"Jesus Christ. A Karmann Ghia."

"I know. I couldn't believe it when my grandson bought it. A German and an Italian Car! We fought both countries in the war. That's two thirds of the Axis powers sittin' right there."

There it was, a red Karmann Ghia with a black top.

Billy walked back into the kitchen in disgust. He sat down and Carwood wheeled back to the table.

"Alright, we'll leave Sunday evening after Margaret leaves the house. That means we have five days to get ready. First, we have to see if the car will start."

Billy wished it wouldn't so they would be forced to find a different vehicle. Unfortunately, Carwood was mechanically inclined and with Billy's help had the car up and running in no time.

They also needed money. Well, Carwood needed money. Billy wasn't going to tell anyone he had almost a million dollars. So, Billy drove Carwood to the bank and Carwood withdrew his savings. He had $23,000.18 to his name. Carwood was transparent about his financial situation.

When they returned from the bank they sat down at the kitchen table and Carwood spread out all the money he had in the world.

"You know, I could just take your money and leave."

"You could but I don't think you will."

"Do me a favor. Don't trust anyone until we're safe. OK?"

Billy shook his head for a moment.

"Wait! What about your passport?"

"I've got one."

"Is it expired?"

"No."

Billy clapped his hands and rubbed them together.

"Alright. Where are we going to cross the border and what city are we going to fly out of? Do you have a map?"

"A Rand McNally. In the garage."

Billy searched through the dust covered shelves until he found it. He walked back into the kitchen while coughing and brushing the dust off of himself.

"Oh, good. There's a map of Mexico in here. OK. We need to get out of the country as soon as possible. It needs to be a busy crossing in a large city. What's closest?"

Billy placed his left index finger on the map just below Lubbock. He drug his finger southwest across the map at a 45 degree angle.

"There."

He showed the map to Carwood.

"El Paso. We'll cross the border from El Paso into Juarez."

"Then we'll fly out of Juarez?"

"Yes. But we'll probably have to fly from Juarez to Mexico City to catch an international flight."

"Sounds easy enough."

"Yeah. Right. Now, we have to figure out how to make myself look like your grandson. I'm sorry to disappoint you but I can't grow much of a beard so that's not going to help us much. I'll have to bleach my hair to get it that blonde. Glasses will help and I'll wear a baseball hat. OK. What else?"

"I think that's about it."

"Oh! Drivers license. Do you have his drivers license?"

"Yes. It was with the passport."

Carwood went to get it. He wasn't smiling when he brought it to Billy.

"It's expired."

"Expired? Damn it! What about car insurance?"

Carwood shook his head no.

"What else do we need, Billy?"

"A bible."

Carwood was hungry. They were so busy planning their trip, they forgot to eat lunch. Billy made Carwood's favorite meal, spaghetti.

"Why is it so important for you to go to Europe?"

"The best men I ever knew are buried there. I want to pay my respects before I die. I would be honored to be buried next to them."

"What did you do in the war?"

"I was a glider pilot."

"Why did they use gliders?"

"You can't hear a glider. Planes make a lot of noise. If you want to sneak up on the enemy or get behind enemy lines, you don't want to make a lot of racket."

"Why didn't you just parachute?"

"Men get separated easily when they parachute. A glider can carry thirteen men and their equipment. They could even carry a jeep and a howitzer if need be. Three successfully landed gliders would provide a well-armed platoon."

"And we trained right here in Lubbock."

"In Lubbock?"

"Yep, at the South Plains Army Air Field out by the airport. Almost all of the glider pilots in the war trained there. Not much left of it now though. After Pearl Harbor was attacked, we were all gung ho to sign up. I went to the enlistment office downtown. I wanted to be a fighter pilot but they wouldn't have me because of my eyesight. Luckily, I went to school with the enlistment officer at the airfield and he got me in as a glider pilot. I guess he figured it didn't matter since they were designed to crash land anyway."

Carwood looked at the kitchen clock. It read 6:35.

"Damn it. Wheel of Fortune is on."

Carwood abruptly left the table. Billy washed the dishes and then joined him in the living room.

Billy stopped guessing the answers because it would piss Carwood off when he solved the puzzle. He wasn't really paying attention anyway. His mind was still racing and he really wanted to smoke some weed.

The next day Billy walked to Target to get some important items for the trip. He didn't want to drive. He'd rather walk than risk getting pulled over by some Barney Fife.

The Target optometrist was puzzled when Billy wanted to buy a pair of glasses with nonprescription lenses in them. He also went to the hair care section for some blonde hair dye. He was not excited about this part of the plan.

"This ought to be fun."

He was thoroughly embarrassed when the cute girl at the checkout counter told him she used the same product to color her hair. His next stop was a fast food Mexican restaurant, Taco Villa. Carwood asked his to stop there and get some bean burritos.

"Oh, man. I wish I had some weed. Smoke a bowl and then eat some Mexican food. Yummy."

Carwood was excited when Billy got home and quickly scarfed down his lunch. Margaret always wanted him to eat healthy and would never bring him fast food.

"Make sure you take out the trash before Sunday. I don't want her bitchin' at me for eating Taco Villa."

Billy dumped his Target bag full of purchases on the table. He sat down and began reading the instructions for the hair dye.

"What do you have there?"

"Hair dye."

"Well, blondes do have more fun."

"Ha. Ha."

"His hair was almost white when he was a little boy."

"Where is your grandson?"

"He passed on."

"I'm sorry."

"He and his father died in a plane accident. Richard was teaching him how to fly and something went wrong with the plane."

"Oh, man."

"Ronnie and I were going to Europe together after he graduated from high school. Well, when he and Richard died I didn't have anyone to take me."

"Wait. Your son's name was Richard Nixon?"

"I didn't know Nixon was going to be president!"

"Alright. Take it easy. Do you have any other family besides Margaret?"

"None I care to talk to. My wife passed away a lustrum ago."

"How about you, Billy? You got any family?"

"My parents. I'd like to let them know I'm alright but it's too risky to contact them."

　　Carwood started sifting through the items on the table.

"Why did you buy a notepad?"

"I need to practice signing Ronnie's name. And I want you to start calling me Ronnie from now on."

"Alright, Ronnie. But why do you need to sign his…I mean your name?"

"If some official doesn't believe I'm your grandson, being able to forge your grandson's signature may be the only way I can fool him."

"Good thinkin'. Well, I'm gonna go take a nap."

"Alright. See you at dinner."

"Will you make spaghetti again?"

"Again?"

"I like spaghetti."

"OK."

　　Carwood retired to his room and Billy started practicing Ronnie's signature. He filled three pages with signatures before his hand started cramping.

"Ugh. A nap sounds like a good idea."

Billy retired to his room.

　　Billy dreamt of being interrogated and arrested at the airport. In his dream, he was asked for his birthdate, social security number and zodiac sign. He didn't know any of these things. That's when he was cuffed and taken to jail.

　　As Billy awoke, he quickly realized details such as a home phone number and address were more important than trying to forge a signature. He needed to commit these things to memory.

　　Besides memorizing facts about Carwood's dead grandson, the next few days were uneventful. Billy kept himself busy by working on the yard and cleaning the house.

Sunday couldn't come fast enough for him. Carwood was calm. He didn't have anything to lose. Billy did. His freedom and his life were at risk.

"Well Carwood, this is our last night. How about a nice dinner?"

"Spaghetti is fine with me."

"I saw an Italian restaurant on the way to Target."

"Oh, you mean Orlando's. They have very good food."

"Alright. I shall return."

"I'm going to watch Wheel of Fortune."

Billy made it back before Carwood's favorite show was over.

"I'm pretty sure this is going to taste much better than my spaghetti."

"You're right. Hang on. I've got a bottle of wine somewhere. Look behind the Black Velvet."

"Let's see. Yeah, there is a bottle in here. Llano Estacado, Cabernet Sauvignon. Well Carwood, I might even have a glass of wine with you tonight."

"Sounds good."

While he and Carwood had their farewell dinner, Juan Pedro drove into town. He was on his way back from Amarillo. He had all but given up his search. He knew if Billy made it to Amarillo, he was long gone. Billy could've got on I-40 and be anywhere by now. Tortuga pulled off I-27 and into the McDonald's drive thru. He had no idea how close he was to his prey.

Juan Pedro was eating very hot French fries in the McDonalds' parking lot. Juan Pedro rarely ate fast food. Not catching Billy had him thoroughly frustrated and he could care less about his diet right now. He almost choked on the first bite of his Big Mac when he glanced in his rear view mirror and saw a tow truck pulling the orange Karmann Ghia.

Juan Pedro sped out of the parking lot after the tow truck. He caught up with the driver at the tow yard. The driver told Juan Pedro from where he towed the car and let him search it in exchange for a C note.

Juan Pedro rushed to the Koko Inn. The morbidly obese woman with the lazy eye and the jack o' lantern smile sat behind the counter.

"Well, howdy stranger. How are you?"

That Sunday morning came with a hangover for Billy. He quickly remembered why he didn't drink. Coffee was ready and Carwood was almost finished making breakfast.

"Well, good morning sleepy head."

"Good morning."

"I've never seen a grown man get so drunk from drinking three glasses of wine."

"That's why I don't drink."

Carwood fixed Billy a plate of scrambled eggs and link sausages and shuffled to the table with it.

"Well, are you ready for our adventure?"

"As soon as I get plenty of coffee and some ibuprofen, I will be."

Carwood made him a bloody mary. Billy was hesitant but he drank it.

"That tastes amazing! No wonder people drink these. I feel better already."

Carwood sat down in his wheelchair and maneuvered himself to the table at Billy's right.

"So, Billy…What do you think of our chances?"

"I think they're good."

"Well, that's what we thought when we landed in France. You can plan all you want but when it comes down to it you have to adapt to the circumstances."

"What do you mean?"

"I had no idea what life really meant and how precious it was until D-Day. A Douglas C-47 Skytrain pulled our flying coffin, as we liked to call them, across the English Channel. In all, there were almost 4,000 of us glider troops. Most people don't know that. The paratroopers get all the recognition. I just wish the glider troops were as appreciated."

"Jesus. You were at Normandy?"

"Yep. Well, behind it anyway. We landed, if you can call it that, just behind Omaha beach. Our C-47 got the hell blasted out of it. She sped up to avoid the flak so we had to cut loose too soon. We could be towed at 150 miles per hour safely but we had to be going almost 200 when I released her. A glider might come in quiet but there is nothing quiet about being in one. The wind comes howling through the fabric. Silent wings, my ass. The sound. That roar. That's what frightened me the most."

"What happened when you landed?"

"Exactly what was supposed to happen. Geronimo and I were able to put her down gently and everyone jumped out ready for action."

"Geronimo?"

"Geronimo Jones. He was my co-pilot. Not to be confused with Cartwright Jones. They were no relation."

"Are you putting me on?  Geronimo Jones and Cartwright Jones were their real names?"

"Why the hell would I make up their names?!"

"Sorry.  The names were just weird back then.  I mean, I've never met anyone named Carwood before and I've never heard of anyone named Geronimo besides the actual Geronimo."

"Well, I didn't name him God damn it!"

"Alright.  Sorry."

"I didn't care what their names were as long as I could depend on them and I could.  You land a plane in the middle of occupied France and you don't give a shit if your co-pilot is name Geronimo or Shirley Temple as long as he can land the fucking plane.  Not to sound like an old blowhard, but this trip of ours is nothing compared to war."

"Why did you want to become a pilot?"

"Become a pilot?  Hell, I was a pilot.  I was dustin' crops before I was sixteen.  The first time I saw a plane fly over our farm I was hooked.  All I ever wanted to be was a pilot.  Did you know Tom Landry was a pilot in the war?"

"Tom Landry…the football coach?"

"Yep.  He flew a B-17 Flying Fortress.  His older brother, Robert, enlisted after Pearl Harbor was attacked.  Robert's plane went down in the North Atlantic.  Well, Tom enlisted after Robert was killed.  It was at the Army Air Field, right here in Lubbock, where he got his wings.  He was given a commission as a Second Lieutenant.  Tom was one of the classiest men I've ever met.  He flew at least thirty missions over Germany.  He even survived a crash landing somewhere in Belgium.  They ran out of gas.  I guess Tom forgot to fill her up before they took off."

Carwood chuckled.

"He was the best coach the Cowboys ever had.  That son of a bitch, Jerry Jones, fired him.  The Cowboys ain't been the same since."

There was finally a lull in the conversation and Billy took advantage of it.

"Thank you for breakfast and the bloody mary."

He quickly got up and washed his plate.

"You want to watch some football?  I think the Cowboys are playing today."

Carwood slowly wheeled himself into the living room.  He waited for Billy to turn the TV on.

"This is going to be a good game.  The Cowboys are playing the Redskins."

Billy went to his room and started packing.  He realized his hands were shaking as he was folding his clothes.

"I wish I had some weed."

He finished packing and then pulled his duffel bag down from the top of the closet. He stepped over to the door and locked it. Billy took a roll of duct tape out of the Target sack and began taping the stacks of cash around his legs and abdomen. Loose fitting jeans and an extra-large black t-shirt help conceal the money. Satisfied with his work, Billy joined Carwood in the living room.

"How's the game?"

"Damn Redskins are winning."

"You packed and ready to go?"

"Yep. Suitcase is in my closet."

"Good."

Billy stretched out on the couch and quickly fell asleep.

"Wake up! Margaret is here!"

Billy rolled off the couch and stood up. He slapped himself in the face to wake up and walked towards the front door.

"Hello Ms. Nixon. How are you?"

"I'm just fine, John. How are you?"

"Doing fine. Doing just fine."

"How is Carwood treating you?"

"We've been getting along well. He's been telling me about his time in the service."

"I'm sure he has. These days, that's all he talks about."

"Well, would you mind giving me a hand with the groceries?"

"Of course. I can get the groceries if you'd like to visit with Carwood."

"Well, thank you John. You are such a gentleman."

"I try."

"Carwood? Carwood? Where are you? Oh, there you are. I thought you were hiding from me for a moment."

"If only I could."

"Carwood! That's not a very nice thing to say. I only want to help you. You know that."

"I do but somehow you make it annoying."

"How is it going with John.  I know I certainly like him."

"He's OK.  He doesn't bother me much."

"Well, from you, that's a seal of approval."

"Margaret…All joking aside, I want you to know I appreciate how you've looked after me and kept me out of a nursing home all these years.  You're a good sister and I love you."

"Carwood Nixon!  You do have a heart.  I love you too, you ornery thing."

Carwood locked the wheels to his chair and moved the foot rests out of the way.  He slowly stood up and put out his arms.  Margaret moved forward and hugged him.  Carwood returned her embrace.  He wanted to tell her he was going to miss her but said nothing.  Margaret helped ease him back into his chair.

"See you next week, Margaret."

"See you next week, Carwood."

She walked back into the kitchen as Billy finished unloading the groceries.

"You've had some effect on him, Mr. Smith.  I can't remember the last time he hugged my neck.  Well, whatever you're doing, keep it up.  I'll see you next Sunday."

"I'll do my best.  Thank you for the groceries.  See you next Sunday."

Billy walked Margaret to the front door and opened it for her.  He went to the window and watched here as she walked down the steps to the driveway.  Margaret got into her car.  She looked in the rear view mirror to check her makeup.  Her mascara was acceptable.  So was her blush.  But her lipstick was not up to her standards.  She fumbled through her purse to find her favorite shade of lipstick, red.  Billy became more and more impatient.

"Is she gone?"

"No.  She's doing her God damn makeup."

Carwood leaned his head back and loudly sighed.

"Damn it, Margaret."

After applying her lipstick and nodding her approval it was time to check her hair.  Margaret cupped her hands and used them to shape her backcombed with hair.  Once that was to her liking, she started her car and drove away.

"Finally…shit."

He turned and looked at Carwood with a gleam in his eye.

"Alright, let's get the hell out of Dodge."

With an adrenaline rush starting, Billy dashed to Carwood's room. He grabbed the old tan Samsonite suitcase from the closet. Carwood had packed lightly. There were a few changes of clothes, toiletries, a light jacket and a few items of great importance to him. Perhaps the most important was a sterling silver framed black and white photograph of an attractive young woman, his wife Hazel. There were two wallet sized cases. Inside one was the Purple Heart. Inside the other was the Bronze Star. There was a small interior pocket inside the suitcase. That is where Carwood kept his Colt 1911 service pistol.

Billy hurried back to the living room.

"You ready?"

"Yep."

"Let's go."

There isn't much room for two suitcases and a wheelchair in a Karmann Ghia. Billy stuffed the wheelchair in the front compartment and the two suitcases behind the seats. Carwood wasn't much more that skin and bones so it wasn't difficult to maneuver him into the passenger seat. He opened the garage door, drove the Ghia into the driveway and closed the garage door. Billy hopped in the car and glanced at Carwood as he put it in gear.

"Well…ain't we a pair."

Across town Margaret Nixon pulled into her garage and heard a dull thud behind her. She walked to the back of her car and slid the key in the trunk and turned it. As she lift the trunk, a jar of spaghetti sauce slowly rolled towards her. She sighed and shook her head. Fatigue had set in and she did not want to make the drive back to Carwood's house.

"I better take it or I'll never hear the end of it."

Margaret was surprised the lights were already off when she walked into the house. She sat the jar of spaghetti sauce on the kitchen counter and walked down the hall to Carwood's room. She knocked on the door but there was no answer. She slowly opened the door as she spoke his name.

"Carwood? Are you in here?"

Of course, there was no response. She turned the bedroom light on and saw the bed was made and empty. She turned and called for "John". She rushed to Billy's room, opened the door and turned the light on.

Margaret began to panic and called for Carwood. Then she notice the envelope on the kitchen table with her name on it.

At that moment, Billy and Carwood were passing through Brownfield, Texas.

"Alright, Carwood. We've got seven days before Margaret finds us missing. That should give us plenty of time to get across the border and on a plane. Margaret seems like the type to get hysterical and call the police as soon as she finds us missing."

"She'll be fine. I left her a goodbye letter so she wouldn't panic too much."

Billy almost swerved off the road.

"You left a letter! Why? What did you tell her? Did you tell her where we were going?"

"No. Of course not. I told her we were going to the Grand Canyon to mark it off my bucket list and we'd be back in a few days."

"What? You shouldn't have written a letter. Do you think she'll buy it?"

"Maybe. But at least when she goes to the police they won't think I've been abducted or the victim of foul play."

"That's actually not a bad idea."

"I figured it might give us a couple more days to get away."

"Not bad. Well, if everything goes as planned we should be on a plane by tomorrow or at least the next day."

Just as they drove out of Brownfield, Margaret finished reading the letter. She pulled a seat out from the table and promptly sat down.

"It can't be. It just can't be."

Margaret read the letter again. Shaking her head in disbelief, she leapt for the dull green rotary phone hanging on the wall. She dialed three numbers, 9-1-1. An overweight sassy black woman answered the phone.

"9-1-1. What is yo' emergency?"

"My brother has been kidnapped! I need a policeman to find him at once."

"Who kidnapped yo' brother, ma'am?"

"His caretaker. He kidnapped him and took him to the Grand Canyon."

"The Grand Canyon?"

"Yes. The Grand Canyon."

"How do you know they are at the Grand Canyon?"

"That's where he says they went in the letter."

"What letter?"

"The letter he wrote to me."

"Who wrote you the letter?"

"My brother!"

"Your brother wrote you a letter tellin' you he was going to the Grand Canyon?"

"Yes."

"That don't sound like no kidnappin' to me."

"There is no way Carwood would just leave. He hasn't left this house in years. He must have been forced to write this letter! It's a kidnapping. I know it."

"I'll send an officer to yo' house so you can file a report. Is there anything else I can assist you with?"

"Anything else!? My brother has been kidnapped!"

"Like I said ma'am, an officer is on the way to yo' house."

Margaret hung up the phone in disgust. That was the first time she ever hung up the phone on anyone.

"Officer, indeed! Hhm!"

The officer arrived thirty minutes later much to the consternation of Ms. Nixon. She had been pacing around the house looking for clues as if she were a Hardy boy.

"What took you so long? A man's life is at stake."

She flung the screen door open.

"What happened ma'am?"

"What happened?! What happened?! My brother has been kidnapped!"

The strain was more than she could bear. The officer caught her as she fell to the floor.

After being revived by the paramedics, Margaret drove to the police station and filled out a missing person report. She was somewhat relieved when they told her the New Mexico and Arizona authorities would be notified to be on the lookout for a "cute little red car."

Meanwhile, with Carwood as navigator, he and Billy continued their drive to El Paso. Billy kept his speed below every posted speed limit sign. Of course, the Ghia couldn't go very fast anyway. They only saw one highway patrol car and it was parked in front of a truck stop. Aside from having to fill the gas tank four times and having to help Carwood to the restroom five times, they made it to El Paso without a hitch. It was almost 1:00am as they crossed the city limit sign. Carwood still had the same shit-eating grin on his face that he had since leaving Lubbock. He hadn't said much besides giving directions.

"OK. So far, so good. Now all we have to do is cross the border in the morning and get on the first plane to Mexico City. Let's find a hotel."

"There's a Denny's up ahead. Let's eat first."

"I doubt they'll have spaghetti."

"Shut up."

Billy pushed Carwood up to the table and slid into the booth. They were helped by a Mexican waitress. Both ordered omelettes.

"There's a La Quinta behind the restaurant. We might as well get a room there. I swear. La Quinta must be Spanish for behind Denny's. They always are."

After paying for a room in cash, Billy pushed Carwood to their room.

"Luckily, they still had a room on the first floor. I wasn't about to carry your ass upstairs."

"Well, I sure as hell don't want you carryin' me across no threshold. This ain't no honeymoon. Don't you have some hair coloring to do?"

"Unfortunately."

Actually, Billy couldn't wait to get in the bathroom - not to do his hair though. The money was itching him and making him sweat. As soon as he got Carwood situated, he took his suitcase and locked himself in the bathroom. Billy took off his t-shirt and pulled his pants down to peel the money off himself. He stacked the money of the bathroom counter.

"Oh, that feels so much better."

Billy rapidly scratched his legs before pulling his pants up. He took the box of hair dye out of his suitcase and sat it on the counter. Then he stuffed the cash in his suitcase. He grabbed the box off the counter and began reading the instructions.

"Two hours? This is going to take two hours? Shit."

After the first application, he came out of the bathroom. The TV was on M.A.S.H. and Carwood was snoring. Billy slid his suitcase under his bed and gently pulled the remote from Carwood's hand.

"Let's see what's on TV. I've got thirty minutes to kill before the next application."

It was almost 4:00 am by the time Billy got to sleep. Carwood woke him up at 6.

"Come on. Get up. We're burnin' daylight."

"OK. OK."

"I love what you've done with your hair."

Billy grabbed his suitcase and stumbled to the bathroom. He was quickly reminded of his transformation when he looked in the mirror.

"I look like Pony boy."

He took a piss, brushed his teeth and put on some deodorant before taping the damp money to himself again. Carwood was waiting for him when he stepped out of the bathroom.

"Alright. Let's do this."

It was a short drive to the border but it was going to be a long wait. There were a dozen that crossed the Bridge of the Americas but there was already bumper to bumper traffic in each of them.

"I don't believe this. It's going to take us forever to cross this bridge. I'm glad we got gas this morning. And you better not need to pee."

As they slowly made their way to the border, Billy grew more and more nervous.

"This is taking forever!"

"Relax Billy. There's nothing to worry about."

"There's a lot to worry about."

Billy sheepishly scanned the other cars around them. There was a wide variety of vehicles trying to cross the border that morning. There were a couple of buses, a cement truck, eighteen wheelers, sedans, motorcycles, trucks and taxis. The taxis caught Billy's attention.

"Why are all the taxis green and white bugs? What is the deal with all the Volkswagens?"

Mexico is the last country still producing the original Volkswagen beetle. They are cheap and widely used throughout the country, especially as taxis. The taxis have a green body with a white top.

"I'm sick of Volkswagens."

"Me too."

After over an hour of waiting in traffic, the Mexican border patrol agent glanced at them and waived them across.

"That's it? We had to wait over an hour for him to barely even look at us? Good grief."

From the border, it was a straight shot to the Aeropuerto Internacional Abraham Gonzalez. It was only eleven miles away. Billy felt a little relieved.

"We've made it across now we just have to make it on a plane."

"Aeropuerto Internacional Abraham Gonzalez de Ciudad Juarez, Chihuahua Mexico. Now, that's a mouthful."

Billy took the exit.

"Do you see a spot to park?"

"Nope, not a one."

"Is everyone in Mexico flying out of this airport today?"

They found a spot on the second to the last row. Billy pulled the suitcases and the wheelchair out of the car. He managed to get Carwood out of the car and into his chair without too much difficulty.

"Alright Carwood, do you want to be a pack mule or can you push yourself to the terminal?"

"I can manage."

Billy put on a black baseball cap to hide his blonde hair. He stepped in between the suitcases, slightly squatted and picked them up. Then he looked back at Carwood and nervously grinned.

"Let's do this."

It didn't take them too long to get to the terminal. Beggars sat on each side of the sliding glass door entrance. Inside it was poorly lit, dirty and smelled of jet fuel and trash. Just as the parking lot indicated, the terminal was full of people.

"At least with this many people we'll be able to blend in. Let's find a ticket counter. Here, you better let me drive."

Billy stacked the suitcases in Carwood's lap. He carefully weaved the wheel chair through the crowd and stopped at the first counter he found.

"Aeromexico. That'll work."

There were a dozen or so people waiting in line. At the front of the line was a Mexican businessman arguing with an attractive young lady behind the counter. A Federale dressed in olive green fatigues and armed with a machine gun stood about ten feet to the right side of the counter. He was keeping an eye on the irate businessman. From what Billy could tell with his limited Spanish, the businessman was pissed off because he purchased a first class ticket but was given a coach seat. He began talking faster and louder. The Federale had enough and whistled at the man. He gave him a stern look and motioned with his head that he was done and needed to move on. With a huff, he walked away.

The other travelers were not high maintenance or either realized the Federale was now in a foul mood and were smart enough to not test his patience. Billy and Carwood definitely didn't want anything to do with him. It didn't take too long for them to get to the front of the line.

The attractive ticket agent had shoulder length straight black hair parted down the middle. Her skin was light brown and her eyes were dark brown. Billy was enamored but had no time for flirting and getting the hell out of Dodge was his only concern. "Criselda" was on her name tag.

"Hola senorita."

"Hola, como esta usted?"

"Muy bien, y tu?"

"Bien, gracias."

"Necitamos…um…we need…como se dice tickets?"

"I speak English sir."

"Oh, good. My Spanish is horrible, as you can tell. We need tickets to Paris."

"Ah Paris, such a romantic city."

"Well, there won't be any romance on this trip."

"Can I see your passports sir?"

"Yes, of course."

"And how are you two related?"

"He is my grandfather."

She began to fumble through the passports. Carwood kept his mouth shut.

"Let's see, Ronald and Carwood Nixon. Everything looks in order."

She handed the passports back to Billy.

"Let me check and see what flights are available. And what is the purpose of your trip Mr. Nixon, business or pleasure?"

"Pleasure. Going to Europe is one of the things on my grandfather's bucket list so we decided to start our trip there in Paris. Visiting Mexico was also on his list and and flights to Europe are cheaper here than in the states."

"I see. Well, I hope you enjoyed your stay in our country."

"Yes ma'am, we did."

"It looks like there are two seats available to Paris through Mexico City. The flight out of Mexico City leaves tonight and the flight to Mexico City leaves in two hours. Does that sound good to you Mr. Nixon?"

"Perfect."

"Alright, that will be 80,000 pesos."

"We lost our credit card last week and only have our emergency cash. Would it be alright if we paid in cash?"

"Yes sir, we take cash."

"It's US dollars. Is that OK?"

"Yes sir. It will be…4,242 dollars and 68 cents in US dollars."

Billy knew that was overpriced but he wasn't going to argue. He pulled a wad of C notes out of his pocket and discreetly counted the money.

"Here you go."

"Alright, let me print out your tickets and I'll have you on your way."

"Thank you."

"Here's your change and here are your tickets. Enjoy your trip."

"Thanks again."

Billy whipped Carwood's wheelchair around and bent over to whisper in his ear.

"Alright Carwood, let's get the hell out of here."

A slight feeling of relief came over Billy. He knew they were one step closer to freedom.

The security check was just around the corner. They took their place in line. A couple of bored looking Federales armed with machine guns were milling about the metal detector. The security guards were herding people through like cattle but not very quickly. The scrawniest of the bunch was collecting suitcases to put through the scanner.

"This is going to take forever. Carwood, you haven't said much. You alright?"

"I need to pee."

"Pee? Can you wait until we get through the security check?"

"I don't think so."

"Damn it. Fine. Let's go."

"I can't help it. I'm old. I have to pee a lot. That's just the way it is."

"Equipaje."

The scrawny guard was standing next to Billy. He was startled.

"Equipaje. Necesito tu equipaje."

Billy understood and slowly handed him their suitcases.

"Well, at least our luggage will make it. Let's find you a bano."

As they turned into the main terminal, Billy wished Carwood would wear Depends. He was tired of all the pee breaks.

When they returned, the line was much shorter.

"Looks like there's only about nine people in front of us. We're below double digits now."

The guards weren't paying much attention to the people passing through. They were only searching the luggage that looked like it may contain valuable items. Theft of said items was a job perk. Billy wasn't worried about the luggage. He knew he was OK unless they frisked him since the money was taped to his body. It made him sweat and the stress of the moment made him sweat even more.

Billy could see their suitcases next in line for the scanner. The scrawny guard heaved them onto the black rubber treadmill. Billy's suitcase passed through first. As Carwood's suitcase disappeared behind the carwash like plastic curtains, the red light on the top of the scanner began to flash. Billy had a death grip on the wheelchair.

The guards grabbed the mad Mexican businessman who just happened to be passing through the metal detector as Carwood's suitcase was passing through the scanner. They mistakenly thought the suitcase belonged to him. The Federales didn't look bored anymore. They rushed over to the scanner to see what all the commotion was about. Billy watched as they opened Carwood's suitcase and pulled out the gun. A wave of panic crashed over Billy. He stood frozen. The businessman vehemently denied ownership of the suitcase and the pistol. A crowd of curious onlookers gathered. Billy forced himself to move and slowly pulled Carwood away from the ruckus.

"What's happening? Where are we going?"

Carwood couldn't see what happened from his vantage point in the wheelchair. Billy leaned over and whispered to him.

"The just pulled a fucking gun out of your suitcase."

"Oh, no."

"Oh, yes."

Billy got the wheelchair turned around and wanted to start running. Lucky for him, he didn't. Guards and Federales came running towards them. He kept pushing Carwood as they ran passed them. Tunnel vision took over and Billy pushed Carwood straight towards the exit. He knew it wouldn't take them long to figure out the suitcase didn't belong to the businessman. It seemed like an eternity for him to reach the sliding glass doors. As he pushed Carwood out of the terminal, he turned to the left towards the parking lot. He didn't want to but he knew he must look. He sheepishly raised his head and slightly turned his head to look back into the terminal. Fingers were pointed at them and officials were yelling in Spanish.

"Shit!"

Billy shoved Carwood's chair forward and began pushing it as fast as he could. He knew they didn't have time to make it to the Ghia. It was too far away. He had to think fast.

A row of the green and white bug taxis were parked along the curb. They were all running. The drivers were congregated at the taxi stand waiting for a fare. As they smoked and talked about last night's futbol game, Billy stopped Carwood's chair and backed him off the curb. He pushed him to the passenger side of a vocho, opened the door and swung him in. Billy pushed the wheelchair into the street and ran around the car to the driver's side. One of the taxi drivers saw the auto theft in progress and alerted the others. They were yelling at Billy as they rushed towards the novice car thieves.

Billy slammed the emergency brake down and backed into another vocho as they made their getaway. Darting into the street, they almost hit a passenger bus head on. Billy managed to swerve out of the way just in time. The bus crashed into the taxis.

They could hear gun fire as the rear window shattered. A T intersection lay ahead. Billy made a right turn without slowing down. The bug came up on two wheels. It sideswiped a parked truck on the other side of the street and then came down. Billy revved the engine and shifted into fourth gear. There was a red light at the next intersection. He wasn't about to stop. As he ran the red light, he narrowly missed hitting another taxi. Billy took the next exit and merged onto the highway. He kept his speed up and wove in and out of traffic getting away from the airport as fast as possible.

"You better slow down."

Billy took a deep breath and exhaled. He relaxed his grip on the steering wheel and let off the accelerator.

"Tell me Carwood…Why the fuck was there a gun in your suitcase?!"

"I forgot it was in there."

"You forgot there was a gun in the suitcase?! Great! Just great!"

"What are we going to do now?"

"Carwood… I have no idea. But we have to get rid of this car. I never want to drive a Volkswagen again."

"How about a bus?"

"Take a bus or steal one?"

"That's up to you. I'm just along for the ride."

"Well, if I had your gun, I could steal one."

"Smart ass."

"Maybe a bus isn't a bad idea."

The next exit sign read 'Paso Subterrano de la Autopista'. Billy took it.

"What are you doing?"

"A Texas u-turn."

"Texas u-turn?"

Billy stayed in the exit lane and made a u-turn under the highway.

"Are you nuts? We're head back to Juarez!"

"I know."

"You know! Why are we going this way?"

"They're looking for a taxi leaving Juarez not headed to it."

"It's risky."

"Yes, it is. The next biggest city is Chihuahua. If we can get on a bus to Chihuahua and make it there without getting caught maybe we can get on a plane out of here."

Billy merged onto the highway towards Juarez.

"You know…this is the most fun I've had in years. I feel alive again."

"I've had enough fun."

"I do have a favor to ask."

"God, what now?"

"Can we find a restroom first?"

"An enlarged prostate must be a hell of a thing."

"You have no idea."

"I guess a restroom is as good a place to hide as any."

As they drove back into Juarez, black sedans with white stripes down the middle of them and flashing red and blue lights on top sped down the highway in the opposite direction. The white words 'Policia Federal' were stenciled on the sides of the cars. Billy and Carwood watched the Mexican police cruisers as they passed by but neither acknowledged them or said a word.

Traffic became more congested and buildings along the highway multiplied.

"Keep an eye out for bus stations."

"I haven't seen anything yet."

"Me neither."

They did see the airport exit approaching though. Flashing lights from a string of police cars in front of the airport could be seen from the highway.

"Looks like we caused quite a ruckus, Carwood."

"I'd say so."

"There!"

A small, square, navy blue sign with a thin white border surrounding the simple shape of a white bus was bolted to the next exit sign.

"Yes!"

Billy took the exit. The frontage road fed into a large crowded traffic circle.

"This looks dangerous."

"Hang on."

Billy sped up to merge with the traffic as he entered the circle. At the same time, the truck in front of them with no working taillights slowed down to turn right at the next intersection. He slammed on the brakes with his right foot and the clutch with his left. Neither he nor Carwood thought to put on seatbelts. No matter, the old bug didn't have them anyway. Billy's chest collided with the steering wheel as Carwood slammed into the dash. The driver of the truck slowly completed his turn completely oblivious to the near collision.

Having barely averted rear-ending the truck, Billy looked in his rearview mirror and could see a car quickly approaching the rear end of their car. He quickly downshifted and floored it, throwing Carwood back in his seat.

"Jesus Christ! Are you trying to get us killed?!"

"Shut up and look for the exit!"

The second exit came and went.

"I don't see a sign."

"I'm taking the next exit or were just going to make a circle."

The exit from the traffic circle was much smoother than the entrance but Billy lost any composure he had left.

"How hard is it to put up a fucking sign for a bus station?!  I mean…"

"Billy."

"What?!"

"I found it."

"Where?"

"Look to your left."

A number of small, dilapidated buildings lined the street and behind them were parked large buses.  A sign reading 'Central de Autobuses Ciudad Juarez' hovered over them.

"Thank God."

He took a quick left at the next street.  Carwood slid into the passenger door with just enough force to knock it open.  Billy slammed on the brakes with both feet and the bug lurched into the curb as he dove across the inside of the car and pulled Carwood back in.

"You drive like a maniac!  I almost pissed myself!  Get me out of this damn car."

"Sorry, Carwood."

Billy got out of the car and looked up and down the street as he closed the door behind him. There were a few pedestrians milling about but aside from the sudden poor parking job, the gringo odd couple had drawn little attention to themselves.

Carwood was dead weight.  He was no help to Billy who struggled to get him out of the car.  Once extracted, Billy stood him up against the side of the car.  He closed the door and looked up and down the street again.

"Think you can make it to the station?"

"Yes, but not before I get to pee."

"You can't hold it a little longer?"

"No! I can not."

"Come on."

Billy slid his left arm behind Carwood and bent over to wrap Carwood's right arm around his neck. They walked into the nearest alley. Billy balanced Carwood as he relieved himself behind a dumpster.

"Great. Now we're going to get arrested for public urination."

"Just shut up and let me finish or I'll pee on you."

At that exact moment, Juan Pablo was intently listening to an interesting broadcast on Instituto Mexicano de la Radio, the public broadcasting radio network of Mexico. Apparently, there were a couple of gringos who caused a lot of excitement at the Juarez airport. Reports were varied but shots were fired, a vehicle was stolen and the two Americans got away. It was speculated the undynamic duo may have been related or tried to appear that way – a father and son or maybe even a grandfather and grandson. Nonetheless, the two suspects were still at large. The search had been stretched to Chihuahua, Monterey, and Mexico City.

Back in Lubbock, Juan Pablo pulled onto US Highway 62 headed to El Paso.

Billy gently eased Carwood onto a long wooden bench inside the center of the quiet bus station. He stretched as he walked straight to the first ticket counter which was run by the Chihuahua Compania de Autobuses. A balding middle-aged man with Coke bottle glasses slowly doing paperwork sat behind the counter. He looked like a younger version of Carwood.

"Hola, senor. Necesito dos entradas para Chihuahua por favor."

He slowly lifted his head. His brown eyes were magnified as he looked at Billy with no expression whatsoever. Billy wasn't sure if he didn't understand his Spanish or was just annoyed by it. After a moment of awkward silence that seemed incredibly long to Billy, the employee nonchalantly tapped the space bar with his right index finger. He leaned forward until his face was less than a foot from the monitor. His gaze slowly moved back and forth from the monitor to the keyboard as he used the hunt and peck method.

Billy stared at him in disbelief and couldn't help but think of Speedy Gonzalez' cousin Slow Poke Rodriguez. He was in the rush of his life and this human sloth controlled his fate. All he could do was turn around and shake his head in absolute frustration.

After finally getting their tickets, Billy quickly walked back to Carwood.

"Alright, let's get on our bus."

"I need to pee again."

"What? You just peed."

"I need to go again."

"Our bus is about to leave."

"I've got to go."

"Shit. Come on."

Billy got him in and out of the restroom as fast as possible. He didn't even let Carwood wash his hands.

"You can wash them on the bus. Let's go."

There were only a handful of people waiting to get on the bus. Billy and Carwood took their places at the end of the line. Oddly, they were the only passengers without luggage. No one seemed to notice though. It was difficult for Billy to get Carwood into the bus but the bus driver gave him a hand.

"Back of the bus, Carwood."

Billy wanted to be in the back of the bus for a couple of reasons. First, people couldn't look at them if they were behind them. Second and most importantly, they were close to the bathroom.

Carwood was able to support himself using the aisle seats and he shuffled himself to the back of the bus. Billy gently lowered Carwood into the last aisle seat and then climbed over him to sit in the window seat.

"It's a four hour bus ride to Chihuahua. Think you can hold it that long?"

"Probably not."

"Well, give it the old college try."

"I didn't go to college."

"Well, try anyway."

Instead, Carwood closed his eyes and exhaustion got the better of him. With a cautious sigh of relief, Billy leaned his head back and exhaled. He was exhausted but dare not fall asleep. A woman moving to the back of the bus quickly grabbed his attention.

She was a woman of short stature and great width scooting sideways with her hands raised above her head trying to narrow her girth. Billy hoped she was only headed to the restroom. After closing the door behind her, Billy tried to calm himself. He longed to smoke some weed. Then, it suddenly dawned on him that he was now wanted by the DEA, La M and the Federales. His stress level rose.

The bus driver started the engine and the smell of diesel creeped in the windows. As the driver shut the bus door, the squatty woman exited the restroom and sauntered down the aisle to her seat. There was the sound of air brakes and the bus slowly pulled away from the curb. At that moment, the smell hit Billy. The restroom door was open just enough for the smell to escape. Billy reached across the sleeping Carwood and closed the door.

Billy's gagging woke Carwood up.

"What the hell is that smell?"

"The restroom. I think it's been a long time since they emptied that thing."

"I can't sit here for four hours."

"Neither can I."

Billy moved Carwood to the last available row of the bus. He lowered their window as well as the window behind them.

"They should have given us gas masks or at least barf bags when we got on the bus."

"I think I can hold it for four hours. I've smelt the most horrible things in war but that's a close second."

"No wonder no one else sat in the back. Jesus Christ. As long as I live I will never forget that smell."

After the nausea wore off, they began to formulate a game plan.

"We can't just show up at the airport and buy tickets out of the country without a single piece of luggage. That's bound to raise suspicion."

"A warm bath and a soft bed sounds pretty good to me right now."

"Me too."

Billy looked at Carwood. He was pale and had dark circles under his eyes.

"Tell you what, when we get there, let's get a room and lay low for the night. I'll get us some food, some clothes and some luggage. In the morning, we'll go to the airport and pray we can get on a plane and get the hell out of here."

"Sounds good."

Carwood closed his eyes and was soon asleep. Billy felt guilty as he realized it wasn't only his life at stake. There was a frail old man he was now responsible for. It wasn't just about him. He knew that even if they made it to Europe, Carwood was his responsibility until the end.

Carwood's head fell forward. Billy propped him up and leaned his seat back for him.

The bus merged onto the highway and they began their slow trek to Chihuahua. Billy looked up and down the highway. There were no police cars.

Carwood began to snore. He sounded like a didgeridoo. Billy couldn't help but laugh. Then Carwood snorted and woke himself up.

"Where are we?"

"Just outside of Juarez."

"I was hoping we were almost to Chihuahua."

"No such luck.  You only dozed off for a little while."

"Did I snore?"

"Just a little."

"Did you have anything special in your suitcase?"

"No."

"I did."

"Like what?"

"My medals and a picture of my wife."

"And your gun."

"Smart ass.  If we can, I'd still like to fly to Paris."

"Why Paris?"

"I want to visit an old friend of mine."

"In Paris?"

"No.  He lives in Traves, a village in eastern France."

"Did you know him during the war?"

"Yes."

"Are you sure he's still alive?"

"Yes.  He's still alive."

"And how are you going to explain me?

"You're my grandson."

"I haven't seen him since 1945.  He knows nothing of my son or grandson."

"Carwood, I'm impressed.  I didn't know you had any friends."

"Had is right.  Not many of 'em left."

"Don't make any plans for social calls just yet.  We've got a long way to go."

"Oh, we'll make it.  Just relax."

"Relax?  I'll relax when my feet are on the European continent."

"You'll love it. So many countries, languages and cultures. I'll be glad to see it again before I die."

"How old are you Carwood?"

"Eighty years young."

"Well, don't go dyin' on me. You're the only friend I've got."

Carwood fell asleep shortly after the bus left and slept the rest of the way. Billy stayed awake. He was still on edge.

"Chihuahua, Chihuahua. Wake up Carwood. We're here."

"Already?"

"I must be boring company. You slept almost the whole way here. Lucky for you and for me, I stayed awake. I saw the airport on our way in. We're not far from it. There are some hotels down the street. Let's go find a room and get something to eat."

"I'm game."

Billy helped Carwood off the bus and down the street. They went into the first hotel they found, Hotel Occidental.

"Does that sign say Hotel Accidental?"

"No, Occidental. But accidental is more accurate."

The front door was a single piece of full-length glass. At the bottom right corner of the door, the glass was cracked in the shape of a large spider web. The damage appeared to be from a baseball. Full-length glass windows bordered each side of the front door. Dark green curtains were open and let in the light of the late afternoon. Three wooden chairs were the only furniture in the small lobby.

Unfortunately for the weary travelers, the only available room was on the second floor. Billy tried to hide his annoyance but it was obvious this most recent obstacle frustrated him.

"At least it's not on the third floor."

Billy cut his eyes at him.

"Shut up."

They were both out of breath when they made it to their room. Billy laid Carwood on the bed and sat down next to him.

"Shit. There's only one bed. I told her we needed two beds."

"Looks like we're bunkmates."

"Great. Just don't play your didgeridoo tonight."

"My what?"

"Never mind.  Get some rest.  I'm going to get us some food."

"Can you help me to the toilet first.  I've got to pee."

"Of course, you do."

After assisting Carwood to the bathroom and back to the bed, Billy checked to make sure the key was in his pocket.

"Don't answer the door for anyone."

He locked the door and closed it behind him as he stepped into the hallway.  Before walking to the stairwell, he glanced up and down the hallway.  There was no one in the hallway.  Billy made his way down the stairs, through the lobby and out into the street.

It had been a long day for Billy and Carwood and it was almost over.  There was a beautiful sunset occurring deep in the heart of the Chihuahuan Desert.  If Billy was just a few blocks over, he would have been able to see the blend of pink, red, yellow and orange rays of light piercing through the few low lying clouds hovering above the sunbaked earth strewn with cactus and rock.

Even if Billy could see it, it would have been wasted on him.  Billy could care less about the majesty of nature at this moment.  They should have been on a plane half way to Europe by now but had only traveled 230 miles to Chihuahua by bus - a slow start.

He didn't have to go far to find dinner.  There was a short hunched over old woman selling street tacos on the corner.

"Cuatro, por favor."

"Si."

As hungry as he was, he figured Carwood could handle two tacos as well.  He also got them two Cokes to go, which in Mexico is a Coke poured into a plastic sandwich bag dispensed with a straw.  This confused Carwood when Billy handed him one.

"What is that?"

"It's a Coke."

"Why is it in a plastic bag?"

"The don't use aluminum cans or disposable cups in Mexico.  They recycle everything.  If you want a Coke to go, you get it in a bag with a straw.  You're welcome."

"I'm not ungrateful…just confused.  I had no idea life here was so much different than in America.  This is a very poor country."

"And corrupt. We need to leave this country as soon as possible. Eat up. I'm going to get us some clothes and luggage."

Billy retraced his steps to the taco vendor and crossed the street. The sidewalks grew busier as Chihuahuans left their homes after siesta to socialize, eat, drink and shop. He weaved through the growing crowd looking for any kind of store. Then he saw a name he recognized.

"Woolworth? I didn't think there were any Woolworth stores still open."

A surprised Billy got a shopping cart and made his way up and down the aisles getting what he and Carwood needed. He stood a foot taller than anyone in the store and his bleach blond hair was sneaking out from under his hat. A few shoppers took notice of him but thought him peculiar not suspicious. Billy felt suspicious nonetheless and made his way quickly through what he thought must be the last Woolworth's left in existence.

After checking out, Billy stopped at the department store exit and stuffed the two suitcases he bought with the items he purchased for himself and Carwood. Now he had to manage the crowd on the sidewalk with two full suitcases. Billy shuffled along the storefronts trying to avoid people but it was difficult while carrying the luggage.

Hoping to avoid attention, he pretended to window shop as he made his way back to Hotel Occidental. It was now dark and the lights from the shops actually accentuated his Anglo appearance.

Fortunately for him, he walked by a farmacia that just happened to be displaying wheelchairs, walkers and canes. Billy's eyes opened wide as he stared at one of the most important things he forgot to get. He quickly stepped inside. Billy sat down the suitcases and pulled the wheelchair out of the window display, paused and then pushed it back. He bought a collapsible walker instead.

Pushing a walker with two suitcases on it down the sidewalk was anything but inconspicuous.

"What the hell is that? Couldn't you find a wheelchair?"

"No. But this is better."

"Better? How is that better than a wheelchair? I can barely walk."

"Just hear me out."

Carwood was not pleased but understood Billy's logic. The authorities were looking for two men, one in a wheelchair. If Carwood could use a walker instead of a wheelchair just long enough to get on a plane, it would help them escape. It was risky. Carwood was weak and could easily collapse if his legs gave out on him. That would draw more attention than him being in a wheelchair.

"OK. I'll do it. No promises though. I might drop like a sack of potatoes."

"Thank you, Carwood. Thank you."

"Billy…"

"Yes?"

"I need to pee."

"Of course you do."

Once Billy got Carwood in bed, the frail old man fell fast asleep. Billy wasn't that lucky. He was back in Mexico and terrified. Their day had been so stressful and chaotic and Billy was running on fumes. He thought he heard footsteps and jumped out of bed. He tiptoed to the door and listened carefully. He undid the latch and slowly opened the door. It creaked and made Billy grind his teeth in frustration. As the door slowly opened, Billy peered out. No one was there. He opened the door wider and looked down the hallway. In the shadows sat a black cat with squinted yellow eyes staring at Billy.

"Black cat. That's appropriate."

Billy closed the door and locked it. He turned around and leaned his back against it. His eyes closed as he rest his head on the door. He exhaled deeply.

"I'm not cut out for this."

He crawled back in bed trying not to disturb Carwood.

"We'll make it Billy. Get some sleep."

"I hope you're right."

"I am."

"I can't sleep. I feel like everyone in Mexico knows who I am."

"Don't flatter yourself. You're not that important."

"I don't feel important. I feel hunted."

"What do you mean?"

"There is a man who works for the Mexican mafia. His name is Juan Pablo. He is there most deadly assassin. I know he's looking for me. I just know it."

"You think they would waste their time trying to find you?"

"How much do you know?"

"Enough to put them all away for a very long time."

"I don't know. Maybe I'm wrong. You might be important enough to hunt down."

"Shut up."

"Get some sleep."

The sound of a rooster crowing woke Billy the next morning.

"Rise and shine, Carwood."

"Huh?...Wha?...What time is it?"

"5:00 am."

"Why are we getting up so early?"

"Early bird gets the worm.  I thought old people always woke up early.  Come on, I'll help you to the bathroom."

After helping Carwood perform his necessaries and getting him dressed in his new clothes from Woolworth's, Billy quickly packed their suitcases.

"You ready?"

"Ready as I'll ever be."

"I'm going to help you downstairs and then I'll come back and get our suitcases."

It was much easier getting Carwood down the stairs than up.  The lobby was empty and only a small lamp on the counter provided light for the room.  Billy sat Carwood down in one of the rickety wooden chairs by the front door.  The curtains were shut.  Billy unlocked the deadlock on front door and poked his head out to look up and down the street.  There was no one on the sidewalk or cars on the street.

"It's dead outside.  We'll have to find a bus or a taxi to get to the airport.  Let me get our stuff and then I'll find us a ride."

Moments later, Carwood could hear Billy clumsily carrying their luggage down the stairs and then the sound of his new walker tumbling to the floor of the lobby.  Billy cussing under his breath was audible as well.

"I knew that was going to happen."

"And it did."

"Shut up."

Billy poked his head out the front door and looked side to side.

"Lock the door behind me."

Carwood leaned over and locked the door as instructed. He sat quietly in the poorly lit room.  A chill in the air caused him to shiver.  He wished he had some coffee.  Carwood thought of Margaret and how she would worry when she found them gone.  He felt guilty.  Unbeknownst to him, she was already worried sick.

A couple of quiet taps on the door caught his attention.   He leaned over again and unlocked the door. Billy pushed it open.

"I got us a taxi.  Let's go."

Billy helped Carwood up and out of the door.  Outside waited a tan Chevy Impala.

"What?  No Volkswagen?"

"Thank God.  I told you, I'm done with Volkswagens."

After getting Carwood situated and throwing their things in the trunk, they were on their way.  The airport was only a short drive away.

"Alright, Carwood.  When we get to the airport, you've got to use the walker.  I can't handle the suitcases and you at the same time.  OK?"

"I can manage."

"You don't have a choice."

"I fought the Nazis.  I can handle this."

It was still dark when they arrived at the airport.  Billy got Carwood's walker ready for him and pulled him out of the car.  He grabbed their suitcases and gave the driver a twenty.  Billy, holding a suitcase in each hand, stood next to Carwood and looked down at him.

"Time to shine, Carwood.  Time to shine.  I'll follow you."

Billy was pleasantly surprised and relieved when he saw Carwood smoothly maneuvering the walker. They slowly made their way into the empty terminal.

"There are some seats over there."

After getting Carwood seated, Billy folded the walker and slid it under their seats out of sight.

"Looks like we're the only ones here."

"Yep."

"How are you feeling?"

"Tired…weak."

"Me too.  The good news is I haven't seen any wanted posters with our pictures on em'."

"That is good news."

"You want some coffee?"

"Yes."

"Wait here. I'll get us some."

"Where am I going to go?"

"True."

"Do you need to use the restroom."

"No."

"Now, that's a surprise."

Billy quickly turned away before Carwood could retort. As Billy looked for some coffee, Carwood reflected on his life. He thought of his time in the service, the tragic death of his son and grandson and his wife and her lost fight against cancer.

The excitement of the past few days was the most alive he had felt in years. He knew he wasn't long for this world. This would be his final chapter and he was at peace with that.

A few travelers and flight attendants walked into the terminal, their voices echoing in the large empty space. Carwood watched them as Billy returned without any coffee.

"Nothing is open."

"I'd rather have a plane ticket than a cup of coffee."

"Me too. The ticket counters should be open soon."

The ticket counter did not open soon. It took over an hour for someone to arrive. Billy felt every agonizing minute go by.

A middle-aged man took his spot behind a large computer monitor. Billy wanted to run to the counter but resisted the temptation. He walked as nonchalantly as he could to the counter.

The ticket agent had thick black hair with hints of gray. He slowly typed on the keyboard and did not acknowledge Billy's presence. After a few seconds, Billy cleared his throat to get the man's attention. He kept typing. Billy cleared his throat again, this time even louder. The agent sighed, lifted his head and made eye contact with Billy. He squinted his eyes and studied Billy. The he smirked.

"Necitamos dos ticketas por favor."

"De donde?"

"Paris."

"No tickets are available."

The agent's English surprised Billy.

"London?"

"No, senor."

"Amsterdam?"

"Si."

"And who is the second ticket for?"

"Mi abuelo."

"Does he need a wheelchair?"

"No, sir."

"He needed one yesterday."

He knew who they were.

Billy stared at the man in misbelief. Where Billy's face showed the unmistakable outline of panic, the other's held no expression.

"Tickets to Amsterdam are very expensive."

"Si, senor."

Reaching under his shirt, Billy peeled back the tape holding a stack of 100s against his rib cage. He pulled the money free and slid it across the counter leaving his hand on top of it to cover the bribe. His corrupt benefactor's hand hovered over Billy's and their fingertips touched as the money was exchanged much to Billy's disgust.

As the tickets slowly printed, Billy realized how dry his mouth was and how much he was sweating. He turned to check on Carwood and was mortified to see two Federales walking behind his elderly travel companion. Averting his gaze, Billy turned to face his opportunistic benefactor who was slowly typing on his keyboard. The ticket agent saw the Federales as well. If they discovered the odd couple, the agent still had an out. He could simply claim the young American fugitive was trying to bribe him.

The Federales took no interest in Carwood. The tickets finished printing and he placed them on the counter without even looking at Billy. Ready to be done with this unsettling transaction, Billy grabbed the tickets and walked to Carwood.

"Come on. Let's go. Don't say a word."

He picked up their suitcases and Carwood dutifully followed behind him. They made their way to the security check and waited for people to get in line. Without a gun in a suitcase this time, clearing security was not a problem. Billy found the KLM Royal Dutch Airlines gate and they sat in the back of the waiting area. They were the first passengers to arrive.

There were no federales, policia or security in sight. The only people near them were two attractive flight attendants gossiping at the entrance to the jetway. The plane was not there yet.

Billy patted Carwood on the back to reassure him. Carwood's shirt was wet with sweat. He sat hunched over and took deep labored breaths.

Passengers began to arrive and took little notice of the duo who appeared to be grandson and grandfather. The noise level grew as the number of people and conversations began to increase. Billy strained to eavesdrop in case they were being talked about but to no avail. His Spanish was too poor and they talked too fast for him to understand anything but a few random words.

Carwood had not walked that much in years and was very fatigued. He fell asleep from the exertion and was lightly snoring. Billy couldn't fall asleep if he wanted to.

The plane was still not at the gate. An announcement was made overhead and their fellow passengers grew agitated. Billy knew this was not good news. He watched as the other passengers picked up their suitcases and began walking towards the main terminal. Billy nudged Carwood awake.

"What's going on?"

"I don't know. Maybe they're changing gates."

Billy looked at Carwood.

"We've got to go with them Carwood. I know your tired but I need you to walk."

"Help me up."

Carwood was dead weight as Billy pulled him up and stood him up in front of his walker. Neither of them were sure he was going to be able to walk or even stand on his own.

"You got it?"

"Yeah, I got it."

Billy slowly let go. Carwood swayed a little but then steadied himself.

"I'm OK."

He picked up the suitcases and Carwood slowly followed him. Billy kept a close eye on the passengers as they walked away. Carwood could only walk as far as the next gate before having to rest. Billy helped him into a seat.

Much Billy's relief, the passengers stopped at a gate three away from their original departure gate.

"They've only moved three gates down."

Carwood said nothing.

"Carwood. How are you feeling?"

"Not so good. My legs are so weak."

"You've only got two more gates to go and then we can get on the plane."

Billy looked outside and could see a large blue and white airplane taxiing to the new gate. KLM was painted in large blue capital letters on the tail of the plane.

"Come on Carwood. We've got to go. Our plane is here."

"OK."

He struggled but slowly made it to the second gate.

"Billy, I need to rest."

"OK, Carwood. Here, I'll help you set down."

Billy watched their gate and saw what he wanted to see and what he didn't want to see. He leaned down and whispered in Carwood's ear.

"We've got to go. They're boarding the plane. We've got to go now."

Billy knelt in front of him and looked him in the eye.

"Look at me Carwood. I'm not leaving you here. Don't quit on me."

"You callin' me a quitter? I outta' whoop your ass in front of all these people. I'd like to see you do this when you're my age. Help me up you son of a bitch."

The last passenger was boarding as Billy steadied Carwood in front of his walker. Billy rushed to the gate.

"Por favor espera! Mi abuelo viene. Por favor espera."

A startled flight attendant turned to see Billy standing in front of her. He was pointing at Carwood.

"Por favor espera. Mi abuelo viene."

"Si,si. Esperaremos."

"Muchas gracias."

He put down their suitcases and helped Carwood to the gate. Billy gave the flight attendant their tickets and they entered the jetway. Carwood moved forward slowly but steadily. Once aboard the plane, Carwood left his walker. Billy took Carwood's left arm and wrapped it around his neck. He grabbed Carwood by the waist with his right hand and helped him to his seat. They both collapsed in their seats. A flight attendant stored their luggage overhead for them.

They had drawn attention to themselves with Carwood's difficulty but Billy didn't care. They made it on the plane and in minutes, God willing, they would be in the air. The flight attendant began making announcements and demonstrated the proper use of the seat belts and air masks.

Billy helped Carwood get his seat belt on.  Carwood looked out the window and smiled.

"It's been a long time since I was on a plane."

"I'd like to be on a flying plane.  What's taking so long?"

"There's a lot to flyin' a plane.  We'll be airborne soon enough."

And soon enough they were.

"Thank God."

Fifteen hours and twenty minutes is a long time to sit in a coach seat but Billy had many opportunities to stretch his legs thanks to Carwood and his Jack and Cokes.

"Haven't you had enough?  I'm tired of taking you to piss."

"Nonsense, my boy.  We're on a grand adventure."

"Well, I have one thing to look forward to…weed."

"Weed?  What do you mean?"

"Weed is legal in Amsterdam."

"Amsterdam is a long way from Paris."

"Oh…I forgot to tell you."

"Tell me what?"

"I couldn't get us tickets to Paris.  Amsterdam was the best I could do."

"Amsterdam!?"

"Shh!  It was the best I could."

"The best you could do?  I wanted to go to Paris."

"There weren't any tickets."

"Ah, shit!"

"Shh!  I promise I'll get you to Paris."

"You better."

"We're not completely in the clear yet.  We've got to get through security when we land.  We have to keep up the grandson/grandfather routine.  OK?"

"Yes."

"Why are we here?"

"Vacation."

"You are a returning World War II vet here to visit…battlefields and…the gravesites of your fellow soldiers?"

"Sounds good."

The fasten seatbelt sign came on and landing instructions were read to the passengers by a very tired looking flight attendant.

"Buckle up."

Carwood finished his drink and fastened his seat buckle.

"This will be the smoothest landing I've ever had in Europe."

Upon landing at Schiphol Airport, Billy asked the flight attendant for a wheelchair. He knew Carwood didn't have the strength to walk and the Jack Daniels he'd been drinking made it impossible. Billy could barely get him back and forth from the restroom.

He thought Carwood's inebriation might actually help their cover story. It was obvious the old man had too much to drink and couldn't walk straight.

Billy pushed Carwood to the luggage carousel and he quickly found their luggage. Then, without even asking, Billy took Carwood to use the restroom. He had learned Carwood's prostate schedule.

"Alright Carwood, you ready?"

"Ready as I'll ever be."

Schiphol Airport is the third busiest airport in Europe and it definitely was that day. Even so, the security lines were moving smoothly. Billy looked at the different security officials trying to decide if a man or a woman, young or old, black or white would be better. He chose to get in the line with the oldest looking security official. The portly bald man with a goatee and glasses appeared to be the most lax with inspecting passports and luggage. He reminded Billy of Burl Ives. They moved quickly to the front of the line.

"Hallo heren. Hoe gaat het vandaag me je?"

"Sorry, we don't speak Dutch."

"Well, it's a good thing I speak English then."

"It seems that everyone speaks English."

"How are you gentlemen doing today?"

"Well, thank you."

Carwood remained silent.

"And you sir, how are you?"

"Well, thank you.  How are you?"

"Very well, thank you for asking.  May I have your passports please?"

"Of course."

Billy handed him their passports.

"Let's see…Carwood Nixon and Ronald Nixon.  How are you related?"

"Grandfather and grandson."

"What is the purpose of your visit?"

"My grandfather is a World War II veteran and wanted to come back to Europe before he dies so that he may visit the places he fought and pay his respects to those who did not survive the war."

The official straightened his posture as he heard Billy's explanation.

"Mr. Nixon, please let me thank you for your service."

He leaned forward and offered his hand to Carwood.  They shook hands.

"Where did you fight Mr. Nixon?"

"Too many places.  The most miserable was right here in your backyard."

"Backyard, sir?"

"The Battle of the Bulge.  It was the coldest and most miserable experience of my life.  I was a glider pilot and we landed just outside of Bastogne this side of the Germans.  We brought the 101$^{st}$ ammunition, food and supplies.  It was a one way trip so we had to fight along side them until Patton relieved us."

"Well, sir, it is an honor.  I and my countrymen thank you."

The official turned to Billy.

"You should be very proud of your grandfather.  He is a hero."

"I am sir.  I am."

"Please proceed gentlemen."

"Thank you."

"Safe travels my friends."

Billy quickly pushed Carwood to the exit. It was a sunny day and Billy stopped to feel the sunlight on his smiling face.

"That was a great story Carwood. He totally believed you."

"He should. It was the truth."

14

Exhausted from the long flight, they wandered around Amsterdam in search of a room. There was a music festival going on and they could not find one. Billy saw a sign for a youth hostel and decided it was worth a shot. He backed up to the door and bumped the door open with his but as he pulled Carwood in. He turned his wheelchair around and surveyed the room. It was a small lobby with mismatched chairs and smelt of marijuana. He approached the front desk where an attractive young Dutch woman with a nose ring, blonde dreadlocks and tattoos running up and down her arms sat. She stretched and yawned as Billy stood in front of her. She was not wearing a bra and her large breasts pushed her nipples firmly against her tight white t-shirt. Billy was tired but not too tired to be aroused.

"Hello. I know this is a long shot but I need a couple of beds for the night. Would you happen to have anything available?"

"Well, you're in luck. I just through a couple of drunk Texans out of here and now have two beds available. Think you and your friend can behave yourselves?"

Billy turned and pointed to Carwood.

"I think I'll be able to keep him under control."

"You do know this is a youth hostel right? Not a nursing home."

"Yes ma'am. We just need a room for the night."

"Well, we only have shared rooms here with bunk beds."

"Bunk beds?... we'll take it. I only have US dollars. Is that alright?"

"Yeah, that's fine."

"Thank you."

"It's 36 dollars a person."

"Here's 80. Keep the change."

"Thanks. You're on the third floor. Stairs are to your right."

"I don't suppose you have an elevator."

"Sorry love, no."

Billy sighed and turned towards the front door. Carwood was slumped forward and asleep in his wheelchair. He gently shook Carwood awake. Billy caught a right jab to the left side of his face.

"Damn it Carwood! I was just trying to wake you up."

"Huh?! What?! What's going on? Where are we?"

"We're at a youth hostel. I got us a couple of beds."

"Oh, good. I need a comfortable bed."

"Don't get too excited. They're bunkbeds."

"What?! I don't want to sleep in a bunkbed!"

"Well, it's that or sleep on the street. Which will you have?"

"Sounds like I don't have a choice."

"It get's better. The beds are on the third floor and there's no elevator."

"What?! This is bullshit."

"Welcome to Amsterdam."

Billy glanced around the room. He saw a muscular blonde-haired blue-eyed young man sitting underneath a window in a worn out brown leather chair.

"I'll be right back."

Carwood watched as Billy crossed the room and approached the young man. Billy spoke to the young man and motioned to Carwood. He arose from the chair and they walked over to Carwood.

"Carwood, this is Klaus. He's going to help me get you to your room."

"Thank you, Klaus."

"Ihr Willkommen."

The former drug courier and the German traveller carried Carwood to the 3rd floor and were able to find a bottom bunk for him. Carwood and Billy thanked Klaus for his help.

"Sichere reisen."

"What did he say?"

"Safe travels. It's ironic Billy. The last time I came to this continent was to kill Germans and now one of them just helped me. It's possible his grandfather and I were trying to kill each other during my first visit to Europe."

"You hungry?"

"Think they have any spaghetti around here?"

"Probably not. Let me help you to the bathroom and I'll go find us something to eat."

After helping Carwood perform his necessaries once again, Billy left the hostel and walked around downtown looking for a coffee shop selling weed. It didn't take long. "Green Place Coffee Shop" was illuminated in neon green lights. Billy went inside and had his long awaited smoke.

The pot in Amsterdam is a bit stronger than what Billy was used to. He stumbled out of the coffee shop and stopped in his tracks. Directly across the street was Bella Ciao, an authentic Italian restaurant.

"I'll be damned."

Carwood was asleep when Billy came into the room carrying the Italian feast and bottle of red wine.

"Carwood, you're not going to believe it. I found some spaghetti!"

"Good. I'm starvin'."

Billy sat the food and wine on a small wooden table in the middle of the room and after helping Carwood to the bathroom they enjoyed their meal.

"OK, Carwood. I checked the train schedules and it's only 3 hours and 20 minutes to Paris from Amsterdam. From Paris we go to Dijon, which is 3 hours and 15 minutes, and then to Traves which is only about an hour. I don't know if we can make all the connections in one day but we can try. We'll get up early and head to the train station."

"Thank you Billy. You don't know how much this means to me."

"So. Who is this friend you are going to see?"

"A priest."

"A priest?"

"Does this surprise you."

"No, well, I didn't take you as the religious type."

"I'm not. Not at all. I've seen enough carnage and evil to know there is no God."

The bold statement took Billy aback.

"OK…well…um…where did you meet?"

"Bastogne."

Billy remembered the conversation with the customs agent.

"Oh yeah, you flew a glider there with supplies for the other soldiers."

"That's right and you didn't believe me."

"Carwood…I didn't know. I believe you were capable of doing it. I just didn't know if you were trying to blow smoke up his ass to get us out of there."

"Elias Janssen is his name. He was studying to be a priest at the time."

Carwood began to laugh.

"Ah, there is no such thing as an atheist in a fox hole!"

"But you said you don't believe in God?"

"I don't. But Elias does and his faith has never waivered…even in the face of those Nazi bastards. He's a better man than I am. He prayed over untold numbers of dying soldiers - even German ones."

"He and his family fled Malmedy to Bastogne. They witnessed the massacre along the way."

"What's that?"

"The SS captured some of our troops and machine gunned 84 of them in a field. Elias and his family heard the Germans coming and hid in the forest. They saw it from their hiding spot."

"Germans are a very thorough people. They walked among the massacred looking for any possible survivors. Any soldiers still alive were shot point blank range in the head or had their skulls cracked open with the butt of a rifle to save a bullet."

"He forgave the Germans. I haven't."

"Do you remember the young man who helped you bring me up the stairs."

"Yes, Klaus."

"Yes, Klaus. I know I shouldn't but I can't help but think bad things about Germans. He's probably a fine young man but the first thing I thought of was his grandfather could have been one of the SS pulling the trigger on a machine gun in that field outside of Malmedy. It's preposterous but that's where my mind goes. His name alone conjured up visions of Klaus Barbie, the "Butcher of Lyon". There's no tellin' how many people that son of a bitch killed during the war."

"Elias and I have something in common. I've never talked about it before. Too painful, I guess."

"I witnessed a massacre too."

"Once we broke out of Bastogne, we made our way to the village of Lutrebois. It was New Year's Eve. I was with a reconnaissance patrol. We made it to a heavily forested hill above the village about mid-afternoon. It was a sunny day so we had a good view of the town. We couldn't make out much though. It was just a quiet little village in a meadow with a stream trickling nearby. Then we heard the crackle of gunfire. Small figures in the distance were being herded out of town, into the meadow. They were huddled together in the snow and then the machine guns fired. A few ran towards the woods but none made it."

Tears welled up in Carwood's eyes and he sniffled.

"That's why I can't forgive."

"Well, Elias moved to France after the war. I don't know how he found my address but when I got his letter inviting me to see him, I couldn't have been more excited. Luckily, you came along. And now I get to see my old friend."

"I had no idea things like that happened. I didn't pay much attention in history class."

Billy studied the frail man's face and thought about all he had seen.

"Carwood, let me have your glasses. They're filthy."

As Billy cleaned his glasses, he noticed how blue Carwood's eyes were – piercing blue.

Billy took Carwood to the bathroom one more time before leaving the youth hostel. He headed back to the coffee shop and then to the red light district.

While he was enjoying himself, Juan Pablo was boarding a plane in Chihuahua.

They made it to the Amsterdam Central Station well before their train was to depart. Billy parked Carwood in his wheelchair next to a bench on the railway platform. He was still short of breath from carrying Carwood down the 3 flights of stairs at the youth hostel and then pushing him to the station while carrying their luggage. Their next mode of transportation was going to be much faster. Billy and Carwood were taking the Thalys high-speed train.

"I can't believe this train will get us to Paris in 3 hours and 20 minutes! This thing goes 300 kilometers per hour. How much is that in miles per hour?"

"About 185 miles an hour."

"What? That's crazy!"

"Hell, our tow target came in faster than that on D-Day. I thought that damn thing was going to rip apart."

"Tow Target?"

"Nickname for a glider."

"Oh."

"We had no motor, no parachutes, and no second chance."

"How many times did you fly a glider in the war?"

"Five times – Sicily, D-Day, Market Garden, Bastogne, and crossing the Rhine into Germany in March 1945. That was my last time in a glider. I'll tell you one thing though. I never got on a glider in combat without an extra flak jacket. That was my seat cushion. I might bite the big one in a crash but I wasn't going to get my ass blown off."

"I think it's time to get on our train. Paris here we come!"

Once they were situated onboard, Billy fell fast asleep. Carwood stared out the window. Memories flooded his mind as the train began to move. The route wasn't terribly scenic but it would get them there quickly. He had been to Paris once during the war. It was the only R&R he ever got.

Paris was liberated on August 25th, 1944. The Parisians were still celebrating when Carwood arrived a fortnight later. Allied soldiers flooded the city. Bars and cafes were full and there were young men standing in line at each of the 177 brothels. The young man from West Texas was stunned by the vibrancy of the city.

The crowds were uncomfortable for Carwood. He enjoyed wide open spaces. A bottle of red wine from a local epicerie and a fresh baguette were more his style. He wandered the streets of Paris with one in each hand. Carwood saw the Eiffel Tower, Arc de Triomphe, and Notre-Dame Cathedral along his increasingly inebriated tour. When he reached the end of the bottle he was standing in line with the other young men waiting for his turn at sexual congress. The wine helped him swallow his pride to avoid dying a virgin.

Carwood was grinning as the speed train pulled into Gare du Nord, the busiest railway station in Europe. Billy was still asleep. Carwood nudged him awake.

"Billy. Billy. We're here."

He stretched his arms high and yawned.

"Man, that was fast. Let me get your wheelchair from the porter."

Billy took Carwood to the toilette before they made their way through the station. It was very chaotic. Announcements were being made in several languages. There was a sea of people going in every direction. Soldiers with automatic rifles scanned the crowd. Carwood and Billy seemed to bump into everyone as they made their way to the next train. The train was delayed. Billy left Carwood and their luggage on the platform.

"You hungry?"

"Yep."

"Alright, I'll go find us something to eat."

"See if they have any Italian food."

"Yeah, right."

As Billy left, Carwood scanned the crowd. He was bewildered at how much had changed since his first trip to Paris. Teenagers with green hair and piercings wandered the station. Businessmen moved quickly through the crowd. Children screamed and cried. It was a different world.

Billy soon returned with a Jambon Beurre – a baguette with ham and butter.

"This is the best thing I could find."

He tore the baguette in half and handed Carwood his share.

"The bread is a little hard but it's not bad. I think I spent twenty dollars for this sandwich and two water bottles. This is worse than airport prices."

" I hate to be a pessimist Carwood, but I don't think were going to make it to Traves today. Hopefully, we'll get to Dijon by tonight."

"I'm afraid you're right."

Billy was right. It was another three hours before their train departed.

Once in Dijon, they stumbled upon a small bed and breakfast near the train station. They had to share a bed but were both too tired to care. In the morning they had coffee and tartines slathered with butter and jam. They quickly gathered their things and made their way back to the train station.

"One more train and we'll be there Carwood. Are you excited? I am and I don't even know the guy. I can't believe we've almost made it."

"Almost is right. I am excited though. Elias is one of the best men I have ever met."

"We've still got a couple of hours until our train arrives. Do you need anything?"

"I could use some wine."

"It's not even noon."

"We're in France and I don't care. Make yourself useful and get me a bottle of wine."

"Well, since you asked so nice and all, I'm certainly happy to get you some wine."

"Just humor an old man, will ya?"

"Alright. I shall return."

Billy soon returned with two bottles of wine.

"I know how you like to drink so I figured I better get a back up."

"Whatever. Just open a bottle for me."

Billy pulled a corkscrew out of the grocery bag and opened the bottle for Carwood. He handed him the bottle."

"Bad news is they didn't have any glasses so you're going to have to drink it like a bum. Good new is I bought cheese and crackers to go with the wine."

"Works for me. You care for a swig?"

"Sure. Even making it this far is an accomplishment. It's worth celebrating."

Carwood handed him the bottle and Billy took a big gulp. He immediately started coughing.

"My God, that's potent."

"Nonsense. It's perfect."

Carwood finished both bottle before the train arrived.

Billy had to help him to the restroom a couple more times than usual thanks to the vino.

Carwood started to nod off just as the train was pulling into the station. Billy nudged him awake.

"Time to go Carwood. Don't let that wine slow you down."

"Shut up and push me to the train."

"One nice thing about you being in a wheelchair is we get first class service."

"Yeah, makes it all worth while…asshole."

"Well, in two hours we'll be there. Where does your friend live?"

"Traves."

"I know that. What's the address?"

"I don't know."

"What do you mean?"

"The address was on the envelope. I didn't bring it with me."

"Shit."

"I'm sure he'll live close to the church. There will be a parsonage or rectory."

"Carwood, you're killin' me."

Billy stared out the window as the wine took effect and Carwood fell asleep. The slow train to Traves swayed back and forth and put Billy in a trance like state. He sighed and was soon asleep as well.

It was dusk when they arrived. Billy got Carwood off the train and pushed him through downtown. Traves was no tourist destination but Billy did find a small hotel for them, Hotel du Mont Blanc. They had to share a bed again and there was a communal bathroom at the end of the hallway.

"Hopefully your friend has better accommodations."

"I'm sure he will."

"Do you need to relieve yourself.

"Yes."

"I thought so. Come on."

Carwood awoke first and tried to get out of bed on his own but his legs were too weak. Billy awoke when he heard Carwood hit the floor. He sat straight up and looked at the empty side of the bed.

"Carwood!"

"I'm down here. I'm alright. I just really need to pee."

Billy rushed around the bed to find Carwood laying on his side and propping himself up with his left arm.

"Give me a hand will ya?"

"Jesus, Carwood, you gave me a heart attack."

"Just help me to the bathroom and I'll be alright."

"I really hope your friend has a wheelchair accessible bathroom."

"Me too."

Carwood and Billy got dressed and checked out before 8am. Billy pushed Carwood to the main street in Traves and then took a right. At the end of a T intersection stood an old church. A small mountain range rose behind it. The sun illuminated the stained glass of The Cathedral Basilica of St. Jude.

"Well, Carwood, that's got to be it."

"Yep, has to be."

Billy pushed Carwood up to the stairs leading to the church. Billy helped him out of the wheelchair and pulled his left arm over his shoulders and wrapped his right arm around Carwood's waist. Once inside the church, Billy sat Carwood on the nearest pew. As Billy caught his breath, he turned to see a large wooden spiral staircase at the back of the church. It appeared to be a solid piece of twisted wood. Billy then sat next to Carwood.

"Now what?"

"We're in a church. Now all we have to do is find a priest."

"What time do priest come to work?"

"Don't be a smart ass. It's a small town. We'll find him."

A portly nun opened the door to the church and peered in. She was puzzled by the odd couple seated in the rear pew at loggerheads with each other.

"Puis-je vous aider messieurs?"

"Oh. Hello. I'm sorry, I don't speak French."

"How can I help you gentlemen?"

"Oh. You speak English. That's awesome. Uh…my grandfather… you see…I am helping my grandfather find an old friend. He is a priest in Traves. His name is Elias Janssen."

"Yes, I know the monsignor."

"Where can we find him?"

"He is in the hospital - lung cancer."

"I'm sorry. Can I take my grandfather to see him?"

"Of course, seeing an old friend will raise his spirits."

"Where is the hospital?"

"It is on the other side of the train station from here."

"OK. Thank you. Come on Carwood. We're burnin' daylight."

Billy helped Carwood up and the nun held the door open for them as they left. Billy quickly pushed the wheelchair back to the train station and then to the hospital. It was a small dilapidated building with an odd odor. The skinny young lady at the front desk spoke little English but was able to understand who they were looking for as Janssen was the only priest in the hospital dying from lung cancer. She guided us down the hallway and to the first door on the left.

There were a dozen beds on each side of the large rectangular room. Small white dressers separated the beds. The bed linens were white, clean and unwrinkled. A single fluffy pillow was on each of the unoccupied beds. There were three occupied beds.

In the first bed on the left side of the room lay a very thin fragile old woman. She lay perfectly still. The sheets were pulled up to her neck and folded across her shoulders. Her mouth was open and her lips curled in because the false teeth were in a small glass on the dresser. Thin backcombed apricot hair covered her head.

Billy pushed Carwood past her. On the right side of the room and six beds down from the elderly woman lay a portly middle-aged man with jaundice. He smiled at them as they continued to the end of the room. In the last bed on the left side of the room lay Elias Janssen.

His appearance surprised Billy. He had thick gray hair and a dark complexion. The priest did not appear sick at all. An oxygen tank sat next to his bed and kept him breathing without too much difficulty. He stared at the ceiling as Billy and Carwood approached.

"Elias…Elias."

He squinted at Carwood and tilted his head as he tried to make out the old man in front of him. His eyes widened and he smiled.

"Hello, Carwood. How are you old friend?"

He stood up out of the wheelchair and almost lay upon Elias as he gave him a hug. It was an embrace between two men who hadn't seen each other in over fifty years who were not related by blood but considered themselves brothers nonetheless.

"I thought I was in bad shape until I saw you."

Elias laughed and started coughing.

"Don't make me laugh. It hurts too bad."

"It's good to see you Elias, really good."

"I guess you got my letter. You sure took your time getting here."

"I had a few delays but my young friend finally got me here. This is Billy.

"Nice to meet you Billy."

"Likewise."

"Billy, would you mind if the monsignor and I had a chance to visit in private."

"No, not at all. In fact, I enjoy any time I can get away from you."

Elias laughed and started coughing again.

"Please, no jokes."

"I'll be in the waiting room if you need me. Nice to meet you sir."

"Very nice to meet you son."

Billy made his way back to the front of the hospital. He smiled at the skinny young lady who led them to the priest they had been in search of since leaving Lubbock. After finding a seat in the corner, Billy leaned his head back and fell fast asleep.

Carwood was not tired. He smiled at Elias.

"Thank you for telling me."

"I had no choice. You made me promise I would tell you. I have to keep my word. I am a priest after all."

"Yes, you are. And I'm sure you've been an excellent priest throughout your career. I'm glad he was found. I just wish someone else had found him."

"It was I who found him and I who told you…but there is still time Carwood."

"Time for what?... forgiveness? I didn't come all this way for forgiveness."

"No, I didn't think you did."

"I can not forgive."

"I can not condone what you will do. I am guilty of orchestrating the sin you will commit. I will pray to the almighty for forgiveness and you must as well."

"Thank you Elias but if there is a price to pay, I will gladly pay it."

"I will ask for your forgiveness then."

"Where can I find him?"

Elias chuckled and grimaced.

"At the fleuriste. He is a florist."

"A what?"

"A florist."

"Well, I'll be damned. "

"Let's hope not."

"How did you find him?"

"He brought flowers to a funeral and I recognized him."

"That's ironic."

"Do you need a place to stay?"

"Yes.  The boy and I had to share a bed last night at the hotel."

"Sounds like fun. Well, it's not much but I know of a small presbytere that is currently unoccupied. You two are welcome to it. It's just behind the church."

"Do you still hunt?"

    Elias knew what he was really asking.

"Yes. I didn't think to hide it. That's my fault. I didn't mean to make your sin easier to commit. Does the boy know why you are really here?"

"No."

"Probably best not to tell him."

"Yes. How long do you have?"

"Six months, six weeks, who knows. I've lived a good life and look forward to seeing all of my amis again. I hope to see you there as well."

"Hhm. We'll see. Regardless, I'm glad to see you again in this life."

"Same here Carwood. Same here."

"Would you like me to bring you some flowers to put on your nightstand?"

"Not funny."

"It was a little funny."

Elias extended his hand to Carwood. They shook hands firmly. Elias grinned and both of their eyes filled with tears. He stood up and hugged the cancer-ridden priest again. Elias shut his eyes as a tear rolled down his cheek.

Carwood pushed himself back into the waiting room. He slowly crept up next to the sleeping young man from San Antonio, Texas.

"Billy! Wake up!"

"Jesus Christ Carwood! You scared the shit out of me!"

"Are you done with your nap?"

"I am now."

"Good. Then help me to the restroom and then you're going to take me to the flower shop."

"Flower shop?"

"Yes. I'm going to get some flowers for Elias."

"Alright."

The young lady at the front desk directed them to the flower shop. It was a small shop in the middle of the main street. The front of the store had a glass door and a single 10x10 glass window to the right of it. "Traves Fleuriste" was stenciled in gold across the window. There were fresh flower arrangements on display perched on antique pedestals. It was a rather chic looking establishment.

Billy opened the door. The shopkeeper's bell rang and he carefully pushed Carwood inside. A old but agile man came from around the counter. He had lost most of his hair. The remaining and now silver hair was neatly cut on the sides and in the back.

"Comment puis-je vous aider?"

The elderly florist had a low gravelly voice.

"I'm sorry. We don't speak French?"

"Well, I'm afraid my English isn't very good. How can I help?"

"I need some flowers to cheer up an ailing friend."

"Ah, well, I have some nice…how do you say?…groups?…arrangements. Here is one. Is old metal pitcher, classic look, very pretty with flowers. These are bleuets."

"Blue ets?"

"How you say?…kornblume…bachelor button."

"Hhm, bachelor buttons, sounds appropriate for a priest. I'll take it."

"Priest? Monsignor Janssen?"

"Why yes, do you know him?"

"Oui, I take flowers to kirche many time. Please tell him I wish well for him."

"I certainly will. How long have you known the monsignor?"

"Couple years."

"Your shop is very nice."

"Merci."

"How long have you lived in Traves."

"Couple years."

"You have a unique accent."

"Oh yes, I am from Alsace. We speak French and German and sometimes a mix of both. The rest of France does not know what to think of us."

"I'll bet. Oh! Where are my manners? I am Carwood Nixon and this is John Smith."

"Nice to meet both of you. I am Marcel Rouser."

"Rouser? That sounds like a german name."

"Yes it is. My father was German and my mother was French. They met during the Great War and he never returned to Germany."

"What a love story that must have been."

"Oui."

"Well, Mr. Rouser, would it be alright if I paid for the flowers and picked them up this afternoon? I want to personally deliver the flowers to my old friend but I need to rest first. It's hell getting old."

"I agree. No need to pay now. Just pay when you return."

"Thank you. I'll be back this afternoon."

"I shall see you then."

"Come on Bil…John, let's go."

The florist held the door open as Billy navigated Carwood's wheelchair out of the shop. They made their way to the rectory. The front door was unlocked. Billy pushed Carwood inside the dark abode and fumbled to find a light switch. Two bulbs in a very plain light fixture lit up the room. There was a small faded navy blue couch and a matching bergere chair with a multicolored quilt draped on the back of it.

Across the room was a small tv with rabbit ears sitting on a short stand. The walls were covered in yellow velour velvet damask paisley wallpaper from the 1970's. A weathered tan braided circular rug lay in the center of the room on the wooden floor. The popcorn ceiling was painted eggshell white. The equally dated kitchen was separated from the living room by a wide doorway.

"This is worse than your place."

"Shut up Billy. And take me to the bathroom."

Down the hallway to the right was the only bathroom, a study and a bedroom. The wheelchair would not fit in the bathroom but Carwood was able to manage on his own. Billy sat on the couch and shook his head as he studied his surroundings.

"How long are we going to stay here?"

"I don't know. I hadn't planned that far ahead."

Carwood wheeled back into the small living room.

"I wanted to take a nap but I don't feel very tired at the moment. I think I'll go get those flowers and take them to Elias and then go to bed early tonight. You can use the bed if you want to nap. You look pretty tired."

"You sure you don't want me to come help you?"

"I'm sure. This little town is pretty easy to navigate."

"Alright. Well, I'm going to go lay down if you're not going to. This trip has been exhausting."

"Get some rest."

Carwood waited a few minutes after Billy closed the bedroom door. He wheeled himself to the study. There wasn't much to it – a few pictures on the walls, a desk, a chair and a lamp. There were random papers on the desk. Behind the desk was a closet. Carwood couldn't get his chair through that doorway. It was difficult for him to stand and walk but he was able to get to the desk and sit in the chair. He took a couple of deep breaths and composed himself. Carwood figured Elias' shotgun was in the closet behind him. He found it propped up against the wall just inside the doorjamb. When he pressed the top lever and bent the barrels down he saw there were no shells in it.

"Damn it."

He brought the barrels back up and closed the break until he could hear and feel it click. Carwood leaned the shotgun against the wall. He began looking through the desk drawers. In the second drawer on the left hand side he found a partial box of shotgun shells.

"Bingo."

When he pulled the box out of the drawer, he noticed something. There was a black textured handle visible in the back of the drawer and Carwood knew exactly what it was. He pulled out the Luger. It was his at one time. Carwood found it on a dead German and then later gave it to Elias as a souvenir. He released the clip and found it was loaded. He wondered if these were the same bullets from 1944. They were.

Carwood tucked the Luger in his pant waistband. He loaded the shotgun and used it as a walking stick to get back to the wheelchair. His breathing was labored as he sat down. With the butt of the shotgun resting on his right foot and the barrel on his right shoulder, Carwood made his way back into the living room. He paused to contemplate what he was about to do.

"Carwood? What are you doing with that shotgun."

He had not heard Billy coming down the hallway. Now he slowly turned the wheelchair towards him and laid the shotgun across the armrests.

"There's something I have to do Billy and I need you to let me do it."

"Why do you need a gun to do it?"

"I'm looking for a person – a very dangerous person. I need to protect myself."

"I don't understand. Who are you looking for?"

"The florist."

"The florist? Why the florist?"

"He was a Lieutenant Colonel in the Waffen-SS. He is responsible for the massacre at Malmedy."

"Massacre? What massacre? What are you talking about?"

"It was during the Battle of the Bulge. They didn't have time to take prisoners so they shot them, 84 of our boys murdered in the snow."

Billy stood silent for a moment.

"You don't need the gun for protection. You're going to kill him, aren't you?"

"Yes. Yes Billy…I'm going to kill him."

"Why not tell the police?"

"He was convicted at Nuremberg and sentenced to death but the sentence was commuted and he only served 12 years. That's not enough. They should have hung the bastard."

"So, you're going to just shoot him in cold blood?"

"Just like he did to my brother and the other 83 soldiers."

"Wait. Your brother?"

"Yes. Henry was part of a convoy headed to join the 7ᵗʰ Armored Division. Peiper's tanks took out the first and last vehicle to stop the convoy. The soldiers only had rifles against the tanks and were captured. Pfeifer ordered all of them to be shot. They mowed them down with machine guns!"

"Carwood…I…I'm so sorry."

Carwood turned towards the door and began pushing himself.

"Carwood wait."

"Don't try and stop me boy."

Billy jumped in front of the wheelchair. Carwood slammed the butt of the shotgun on Billy's left foot. Billy hunched over in pain and then Carwood hit him in the head with the butt of the gun as hard as he could. Billy crumpled to the floor. Carwood gasped for breath.

"I'm sorry Billy."

Carwood pressed the top lever and opened the shotgun. He set the butt in the seat on his right side and positioned the barrels down the side of his leg. He grabbed the quilt and covered himself and the gun. Carwood then left to do what he couldn't stop himself from doing.

He made his way down the sidewalk weaving his way around pedestrians and window shoppers. As he reached the front door of the flower shop, he did not hesitate. The shop doorbell rang as Carwood clumsily pushed himself through the door. The florist looked up from the arrangement he was working on and saw Carwood struggling to get in the shop.

"Let me help you messieur."

"I've got it, thank you."

"That was quite an entrance. Let's see… You wanted the bleuets?"

"Yes, the bachelor buttons for the Monsignor."

"I will get them for you. Follow me."

Carwood hunched over and pushed his wheelchair following the florist. As he went around the counter, Carwood positioned himself in front of the counter close enough keep the shotgun out of site. He coughed as he closed the shotgun.

"Excuse me. My allergies are bad. Say, aren't bachelor buttons also called blue cornflowers and are one of the national symbols of Germany?"

"Ah, you know your flowers."

"Yes, I worked in a flower shop one summer during high school. I picked up some german when I was here during the war as well. Doesn't your last name mean rose in german?"

"You are very astute."

The florist was awkwardly amused and puzzled by this conversation.

"I came to Europe many years ago to fight Nazis."

"Oh, you don't say. Well, I am glad to see you made it home safely."

"What did you do during the war?"

His hair stood up on the back of his neck.

"Well, it's quite funny actually."

He memorized this story long ago and surprisingly only had to tell it a few times.

"When Germany invaded Poland in 1939, I was drafted into the army."

He chuckles to himself.

"I was a horrible soldier. I thought our sergeant was going to kill me during basic training. Well, the day before I was to complete basic training I accidentally shot myself in the foot."

He laughs out loud this time.

"I promise you. I did not do it on purpose. I am just that clumsy. After I left the hospital, I was sent to the mess hall and I peeled potatoes for the rest of the war. Here, I will show you."

He came around the corner and pulled off his right shoe and sock. He presented his foot and there was indeed a wound.

"See, there it is…"

The shotgun was aimed directly at his face.

"Wait! What is going on? Are you robbing me? You can have all the money I have. I will get it for you."

"Don't move! Don't fucking move. You piece of shit! Raise your hands!"

"I will not move! I will not move! Please!"

"Shut up!"

Carwood exhaled loudly and slowly.

"I know who you are."

"Me? I am no one."

"Oh yeah? You're a Nazi. You're a murderer. You are no florist. You are Joachim Peiper!"

"Who?"

"Waffen-SS Lieutenant fucking Colonel Joachim Peiper! You piece of shit!"

Peiper knew he was caught but couldn't stop trying to save his skin.

"Please. No. You are wrong. As I told you, I am French and I was a horrible soldier. Please, look at my foot. I shot myself. I am not this man you think I am!"

"Bullshit. You ordered the deaths of 84 soldiers at Malmedy and one of those soldiers was my brother."

He realized his position was hopeless. Peiper hung his head and shook it. With his sock in his right hand, he motioned at his bare foot.

"May I?"

"Carefully."

He pulled his sock on and put on his shoe.

"Thank you."

"Have a seat."

Peiper groaned as he sat on the floor.

"What about Chenogne? What about the "Take No Prisoners" order?

"What are you talking about?"

"Eighty German soldiers were massacred at Chenogne.  After Malmedy, no prisoners were taken until the end of the war."

"Bullshit."

"I am sorry about your brother. I truly am. If he was anything like you, I'm sure he was a fine soldier. You are a tenacious one. But. We were soldiers. All of us. War is hell. The war is over. I was found guilty and spent my time in prison. I had to lose my identity to live in peace. I've paid my dues."

The shotgun blast almost took his head completely off. Carwood had let both barrels loose. The kickback knocked him out of the wheelchair. The shop doorbell rang.

"Carwood! Carwood!"

"I'm over here Billy."

"Oh, thank God."

Billy looked away as much as he could when he saw the bloody mess that was left of Peiper. Carwood was sprawled out on the floor next to his wheelchair.

"Carwood. Oh, my God. Are you ok?

"Yes, I'm fine. Just help me up."

Billy locked the wheels and help Carwood into his wheelchair. Billy quickly looked him over.

"Are you sure you're ok?"

"Yes! I'm fine!"

Billy hugged Carwood tightly.

"Oh, thank God!"

"God damn it! Let go of me! I can't breathe!"

Billy let go of him and knelt before him.

"I'm sorry. I'm just so glad you're alive. I just knew I would find you dead."

"Well, you didn't."

"Thank God!"

"Stop thanking God! I'm alive."

"Carwood, I just…"

As Billy was about to say something, Carwood elbowed him in the head. Billy reeled to the right side of Carwood. The window with the words "Traves Fleuriste" written upon it shattered. A bullet struck Carwood in the center of his chest knocking him out of his wheelchair.

The shop doorbell rang again. Juan Pablo entered the flower shop. Billy did not realize the danger he was in. His concern was for Carwood.

"Carwood! What happened? Are you alright?"

"I'm shot."

"Shot? Who shot you?"

"He did."

"Hola chivato."

Billy turned to see Juan Pedro advancing towards him with a gun pointed directly at his head. He raised his hands.

"No!"

"Adios pendejo."

Juan Pedro's head snapped back as the bullet passed through it. His body collapsed to the floor. Billy lay perfectly still. Carwood coughed up blood. Billy turned to look at him.

"Carwood! No!"

The Luger slid out of his hand.

"Carwood! No! No! No!"

"It's alright Billy. It's alright."

"Shit. Carwood."

"Damn. I've never been shot before. It fuckin' hurts. It hurts bad."

"You saved my life Carwood. You saved my life. Thank you. Thank you."

"Billy, will you do one last thing for me?"

"Yes. Of course. Whatever you want."

"Take the flowers to Elias."

"Yes. I will take them. Of course I will. I'm going to get help for you first."

Carwood coughed up more blood.

"No. No you won't. It's too late. It's too late for me. Thank you Billy. Thank you."

"Thank you? I got you killed."

Billy held onto Carwood tightly.

"No. You helped me find closure. You helped me avenge Henry. You helped me…"

His head fell back and he exhaled one last time.

"Carwood? Carwood? Oh no. Oh no. Oh no. Carwood!"

Billy held him tightly. He slowly released him and tried to stop crying. He pushed away the wheelchair and laid him out straight. He stood up and turned to see the lifeless corpse of Juan Pablo and the near headless body of Joachim Peiper.

He picked up the old metal pitcher full of bachelor buttons and walked over the broken glass and out of the flower shop. Curious and bewildered pedestrians watched as Billy left and walked towards the hospital.

By the time Billy got to the hospital, an ambulance was on it's way to the flower shop. It should have been a hurse en route. As Billy neared the hospital carrying the flowers Carwood wanted so dearly to be delivered to his old friend, he saw the young receptionist standing outside listening to the sounds of the sirens. He walked past her without her even noticing. Billy's clothes had blood on them and that is the first thing the Monsignor noticed. He was awake when Billy sat down next to him.

Elias had a tracheostomy placed to help him breath easier. It was the beginning of the end for him. Billy could tell he was trying to stay conscious. It was almost as he if had expected a visitor. He sat the flowers on the table. Elias could see that Billy had been crying and knew that all was not well.

"Monsignor...Monsignor, I'm so sorry. Carwood...Carwood was shot...he was shot and he died. He's dead."

Elias extended his shaking hand to Billy. He grabbed it and squeezed it. Billy began to cry and pressed his forehead against the back of Elias' hand.

He stayed at the Monsignor's bedside the rest of the day and through the night. In the morning, the ailing holy man who kept a promise he did not want to keep passed away.

Billy pulled the sheet over the head of the departed. He walked out of the hospital and into parts unknown.

www.ingramcontent.com/pod-product-compliance
Lightning Source LLC
Chambersburg PA
CBHW082048220626
47052CB00007B/1253